A SECOND CHANCE IN VALENTINE VALLEY

A VALENTINE VALLEY NOVELLA

EMMA CANE

OLIVERHEBERBOOKS

Published by Oliver-Heber Books

Cover art by Dar Albert, Wicked Smart Designs

Editing by Jena O'Connor: www.PracticalProofing.com

0 9 8 7 6 5 4 3 2 1

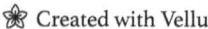 Created with Vellum

ABOUT THE BOOK

"Strong families, deep friendships and sexy heroes abound in
Valentine Valley. I'd love to live there."
NY Times bestselling author Sherryl Woods

Steph Brissette is inching back to life after losing her high
school sweetheart husband in a tragic accident. Between her
family, her work at the Sugar and Spice bakery, and helping the
Valentine Valley widows save an historic schoolhouse, her days
are full. It's only in her dreams that she revisits the accident—
one that she can't quite convince herself was not her fault.

That is, until Jeremy Chen comes back to town.

Jeremy left Valentine for medical school and has now
returned to take his place as the town's new doctor. He first
knew Steph as the bratty little sister of his best friend. Then, in
one heartbreaking moment, she became the woman he saved—
and the widow of the man he couldn't help. Still searching for
his new place in town, Jeremy now sees Steph as a desirable
woman. But can she ever look at him without seeing everything
she lost? The only certainty is that in a town called Valentine,
love is always worth a second chance.

To all my aunts and uncles (numerous as you are!): thanks for reading my books over all these years and supporting my dreams. And thank you even more for the special childhood memories that fill my heart.

1

Stephanie Brissette parked on the small side street in front of the doctor's office, a converted old home with gingerbread trim and a wraparound porch. She got out of her SUV and breathed in the crisp, January air of Valentine Valley, Colorado. Looming above the town, the Elk Mountains were capped with snow, reminding her that she hadn't skied since—

Okay, no need to dwell. She was about to see the new town doctor, Jeremy Chen, who'd saved her life a year and a half ago, but hadn't been able to save her husband. She would get through this.

It was just a physical, after all. So what if Jeremy had been friends with her older brothers, and she'd had a crush on him when she was eleven. So what if he'd been a god to her back then, as he'd led the high school ski team to a state championship. Now he was going to be her general practitioner. It wasn't like he was her gynecologist. *Ew.* It would be fine. She'd think of him as Dr. Chen.

She'd seen him around town since his return, but always from a distance. His smiles had been warm and friendly, but she hadn't approached him. Last week, she'd avoided a conversation with him when they'd both attended a get-together at her brother Daniel's house. She hadn't known how to feel now that he was back, and had ended up leaving early before talking to him. It was cowardly, she knew. He'd always been kind to her. She had to prove to herself that she could take this next step.

She marched up the stairs, through the vestibule and into the waiting room, which had obviously been the front parlor decades ago and was still decorated with overstuffed chairs, quaint old-fashioned frames of the Colorado countryside, and vases full of fresh flowers scattered on tables. Steph knew the flowers were the inspiration of Janet Shaw, Doc's receptionist, who sat behind an antique carved wooden desk. She was the mom of Steph's friend Monica, and she wore her hair in a close-cropped Afro that set off the same stunning cheek bones her daughter had.

Mrs. Shaw looked up from her computer and gave an awkward smile. "Oh, hi, Stephanie."

Steph tilted her head in confusion. "Is something wrong?"

"I made a mistake scheduling your appointment without consulting Dr. Chen. He says he'll explain it to you. Go on down the hall to his office."

Steph followed her directions, then opened the door and found Dr. Chen, who rose to his feet behind the desk nestled between bookshelves.

"Hello, Steph," he said.

Jeremy.

He smiled at her, his hair black and short on the sides but with a longer sweep across the crown. His dark eyes were warm. He wore a long-sleeved green Henley that hugged his torso in all the right places, leading down to a pair of jeans. She quickly realized what she was doing and brought her gaze back to his face. *Where had* that *come from?*

Steph swallowed and asked, "Dr. Chen, what's going on?

Mrs. Shaw says a mistake was made regarding my appointment?"

He winced. "Dr. Chen? Please, you always used to call me Jeremy. And I didn't realize she'd made an appointment for you until I saw it on the schedule this morning. I'm sorry, but I can't be your doctor."

She blinked. "Why not?"

He sighed and briefly looked down at his desk before meeting her gaze. "Partly, I was worried it would make you too uncomfortable. I know I've disappointed you—"

"Jeremy, stop." Everything seemed to settle inside her. Of course she knew how to talk to him—this was Jeremy, always ready with a smile and a gentle flirtation that made her feel special. And here he was, still hurting, too. "You did not disappoint me. You saved my life. You did the best you could, and I'll be forever grateful."

"Then why did you avoid me last week?"

She sighed. "It wasn't you—it was all the memories. I was just taken by surprise at seeing you. I've been doing better, really."

"I'm glad to hear that." He hesitated. "Because there's another reason I can't be your doctor, and maybe it's too soon to say it, but we've always been honest with each other." He came around the desk to perch on the edge.

And then she realized he wasn't looking at her with the air of a man looking at his buddy's little sister. Everyone in their small town knew what she'd been through—no man had wanted to be the first to look at her with interest, as if she was supposed to give off an unseen signal that she was ready to date again.

Without waiting for a signal, Jeremy was giving her a look of admiration, of awareness.

And she wasn't immediately bothered by it.

"We've always been friends, Steph," he began slowly, "but every time I see you lately, it doesn't feel like just friends."

To her surprise the room suddenly felt charged with a different kind of energy. Breathless with the realization that she'd moved into a new area of recovery, she didn't know how to deal with it except to ignore it.

"Wow you really don't want to be my doctor, do you?" she asked with faint sarcasm, one eyebrow arched.

He put up both hands in a placating gesture. "You don't have to do or say anything. I just wanted you to know."

How had he known his feelings had changed? She'd barely given him the time of day since his return. She certainly hadn't sensed a change between them, not until she'd walked into the room, and he'd just...been there, hunky and gorgeous, full of life. And that last thought made her realize how resistant to life she'd been the last year and a half.

"I'm not speaking as a doctor, Steph, but how are you, really?"

"Fine," she said automatically. He didn't look like he believed her, and she felt herself bristling as she added, "I'm not sure how well you're going to do as a doctor when you pick and choose which patients to see."

"Some people are worth being picky about."

"Are you flirting with me?"

"I always flirt with you. But okay. How's your family doing?"

He didn't miss a beat, didn't probe too deeply.

"Doesn't Daniel keep you in the loop?" she asked.

"I'm lucky your brother remembers to eventually answer my texts, what with four kids."

Steph relaxed into a reluctant smile. "Yeah, but he loves being a family man. I still remember when his next tattoo was all he cared about, and I worried he'd be a loner forever."

They shared a moment of companionable silence at the

memory. Jeremy knew everything about her family—he knew everything about *her*. Why did it suddenly seem so different to be with him, especially after what they'd been through together a year and a half ago?

"You're ducking the spirit of my question," he gently chided her.

"I answered your question. The family's fine—I'm fine." She wanted to wince as defensiveness crept into her voice.

"I hear you're working a lot of hours at the bakery."

"I'm a co-owner. That is what one does."

"Officially a co-owner? That's great. You and your sister work so well together."

Steph nodded, distracted from her defensiveness by remembering how hard her sixteen-year-old self had taken it when she found out she had a sudden older sister no one in the family knew anything about. And now Emily was her dearest friend as well as her sister, and had insisted she accept a share in the business that Emily herself had built from scratch.

"Do you mind working so much?" Jeremy said.

"That's why I went to culinary school—I love what I do. Listen, if you don't want to be my doctor, you don't need to be my therapist either."

"Not trying to be. I've just thought about you a lot the last couple years, and I hoped you were doing okay. Are you still competing? I have memories of you racing your horse around the barrels so fearlessly."

"Yeah, well, being fearless led to the worst day of my life, didn't it?"

Why had she said that? They both froze in an awkward, sad tableau of not knowing what to say, how to bring up death and despair.

"Besides," she said gruffly, "I don't have a lot of time to barrel-race. Maybe this summer."

"I hope so. You always loved it."

Doc Ericson ducked his head through the doorway. "Everything okay in here?" he asked. Though Doc was white-haired and retired, his habitual winter goggle tan was still in evidence. "I can come out of retirement for a special patient."

Snapped out of their strained conversation, Steph straightened and turned to Doc. "I'll come set up a new appointment with Mrs. Shaw. I don't want to make Dr. Chen late for his next appointment."

She heard Jeremy chuckle and something inside her eased.

~oOo~

Jeremy stared thoughtfully at the closed door a long time after Steph left. *Barrel racing?* Why the hell had he brought up such an inane topic? She'd been dismissive, defensive, and awkward during their brief talk, but the tension had gradually eased, leaving him a little encouraged that maybe she had felt something that could be more than friendship between them.

He was probably setting himself up for disappointment. Steph was a widow, a cute, blond, athletic, twenty-five-year-old widow. He'd long thought of her as the younger sister of his best friend, and he fondly remembered her bright, inquisitive eyes beneath the ball caps through which her ponytails used to bob. Now, she wore her hair in blond waves dipping below her chin—that she probably still pulled into a ponytail all day as she crafted beautiful wedding cakes, cheesecakes, and cookies. He'd been to Sugar and Spice when he came home from Denver to visit his family, but always seemed to miss her. He hadn't thought anything of it until a year and a half ago, when he'd seen her under the worst circumstance of her life.

A timer went off in the lab across the hall, and the sound

sent him back in time, to when the avalanche beacon ringing through the air had meant life and death.

It had been early in the ski season, and he'd been subbing on ski patrol at the East Vail Chutes. He was a volunteer with Mountain Rescue completing a training op on the hill, paying it forward because someone had saved his brother's life in an accident that had cost him his leg. Not that that had stopped Eric's ski career, Jeremy thought proudly.

He'd been surprised to see Steph and her husband Tyler at the ski lodge a couple hours from home. The two of them had been so wrapped up in each other, so in love, that Jeremy had found himself a little envious.

That afternoon, Jeremy was skiing along the boundary of the resort when he saw a plume of snow rising up behind the white, pine-dotted mountain, framed in a sky the color of a robin's egg. Feeling uneasy, he looked for fresh ski tracks going into the back country and found some. His heart started to pound. He realized with shock that if an avalanche was roaring down the back side of the mountain, someone might be caught in its path.

And then his training kicked in. He radioed his position to the rest of the ski patrol, turned his avalanche beacon to search mode, then launched himself farther through the trees, poling the snow hard to propel himself faster. Almost immediately his beacon was beeping out its distress, and as he approached, it got louder and faster.

The scene that greeted him when he broke through the tree line was the crown of the avalanche, which had fallen away below him. Keeping to the trees, he began to make his way down the edge of the avalanche, careful not to trigger another. At the bottom, he found the debris field, a wide sloping field of chunky ice cubes the size of cars intermixed with real boulders—boulders that could kill. The beeping was stronger now, frantic. He skied forward across the snow that had hardened like concrete

—and then the beeping got fainter. He skied back again, and when the beeping picked up speed, he pulled off his backpack, then yanked out the probe and his folded shovel.

After taking off his skis, he extended the telescoping probe and began to pierce the solid snow. After the third time, with the beacon beeping crazily at his waist, he hit something that wasn't snow and wasn't a boulder. He unfolded his shovel and began to dig until he found a foot sticking out of the snow. Moving faster, he uncovered the prone victim's bright blue snow-pant-covered thigh. They kicked feebly. Was the person suffocating to death because Jeremy couldn't get through the solid ice fast enough? He dug out the upper body even more frantically, heart pumping with fear and focus, that feeling he felt on rotation in the hospital ER.

To his relief, when he reached the head, chunks of snow tumbled down in front of person's face where their arms were cupped protectively. They'd remembered to fall covering their mouth, keeping open an air pocket to raise their chances of survival.

He pulled the victim up onto their knees as they gasped and sobbed.

Stephanie.

Oh God, she wouldn't have been alone.

"Tyler!" she shrieked.

She fumbled at her waist and switched her avalanche beacon to search mode. Immediately, a new faint beeping began on Jeremy's transceiver. He realized there'd been two signals all along, but only one of him.

Exhaustion weighing down his body, he lumbered in his ski boots farther downhill until the beeping picked up speed again. He probed repeatedly, but he was impeded by rocks as large as basketballs that had been flung to the side of the avalanche. When he thought he hit something that gave a bit, he dug as fast he could. How much time had passed? His stomach seized with growing fear. He was used to submerging his emotions while on duty, but Steph sobbed beside him, trembling weakly as she tried to dig with her hands. Her face was shadowed with bruises, her lip swollen and bleeding. She could barely use one arm, she had no shovel, but she kept digging.

"We're coming!" Jeremey shouted, not knowing if Tyler could hear him.

Every second that ticked by seemed to ring in Jeremy's head as if synchronized with the avalanche beacon. He dug until his arms and shoulders felt on fire. As if from a distance, he realized others had arrived, that someone drew Steph away so that more people could help dig with shovels. Her crying and pleas to God echoed in his ears, along with the words in his mind, *Too late, too late.*

Jeremy was the one who uncovered Tyler's limp torso, his blue face compacted in the snow. Jeremy slipped his fingers beneath Tyler's buff and found no pulse. Others helped dig him free, even as Jeremy started CPR, rhythmically pumping his chest, praying for a miracle.

When at last he had to stop, Steph gave another terrible cry and pulled Tyler's into her arms, rocking his body and sobbing. It had been a sight that haunted Jeremy for months afterward. Much as Jeremy could have done nothing different, he felt like he should have been able to save them both.

Had Steph thought the same thing?

Jeremy realized he'd been staring out the window at the distant view of the Elk Mountains, their snow-covered peaks a reminder of beauty and danger. He shook himself out of his memories and went back to his desk to check out the day's schedule on the computer. His first appointment wasn't until 10, so he read through lab results, trying to put Steph from his thoughts, until someone knocked on the door.

Doc Ericson leaned partway through the door. "Steph is finishing up some routine bloodwork. You should be able to leave your office soon."

Jeremy rolled his eyes. "I'm not hiding from her."

"Of course not." Chuckling, Doc sat down across the desk and looked around. "Not used to the view from this side."

"Me neither." Jeremy walked around the desk and took the seat next to him.

Doc eyed him speculatively. "How's it going?"

"Your practice runs like clockwork, so I have nothing to complain about."

The old man cocked his head. "You seem...different. Is the reality of small-town practice making you regret the choice?"

"No," Jeremy said without hesitation. "This was always the plan." Yet Doc had seen through to his unease. It wasn't as if Jeremy hadn't known what to expect as a doctor in Valentine Valley. He'd interned with Doc for many summers in college. But now his laid-back schedule seemed so...permanent.

This strange restless feeling was new to him. Posts online by his Denver friends made him feel wistful for big city life. He told himself it was all going to take some getting used to.

"Plans change," Doc said. "If you want, I could unretire for a year."

Jeremy leaned over and put his hand on the other man's arm. "Doc, you've been good to me my entire life. I want you to enjoy your retirement. Surely there are some mountains in Colorado you haven't skied yet."

"Not many, but I do have a list..." He grinned. "I have some time if you need me—like today. I was happy to help. Any other young ladies you don't want to treat?"

"That just sounds weird. There's not a bunch of women I'm looking to date." He remembered catching a glimpse of Steph through the window of her bakery right after he'd moved home.

He'd come to a complete stop and practically gaped as she waited on a customer, her gorgeous smile making him realize something had shifted inside him where she was concerned.

Doc cocked his head. "You're only young once…"

As the old man sauntered out of the room, it took Jeremy a moment to remember that they'd been talking about his move back to Valentine. He silently berated himself. If close friends like Doc were noticing his restlessness, then he was doing a poor job of controlling his emotions. He'd made his career decision, and he would make it a success.

It didn't help that while he was waiting for his new house to close, he was living with his parents. He was grateful, but it made him feel like he'd gone back to childhood, sleeping in a room full of sports trophies. Besides, he could hardly have disappointed his mom, who relished taking care of him again. He didn't need to be taken care of anymore, but if he wasn't careful, she'd soon be peeling his oranges.

2

After her appointment, Steph drove down Main Street, lined with beautiful old nineteenth century stone and clapboard buildings. A recent snowfall gave the old-fashioned lampposts jaunty hats of snow. Tourists from Aspen strolled arm-in-arm down the street, ducking into restaurants like Carmina's Cuccina, coffee shops like Espresso Yourself, or boutiques like Monica's Flowers and Gifts. As Steph drove past Monica's, she slowed down to look at her own bakery next door, where last week a beautiful new sign had been raised: Sugar and Spice Sisters. She still couldn't believe Emily had made her a co-owner, but the sign made it feel real. She and her sister were responsible for the success of a thriving business, and through the plate-glass windows, she could see customers lined up at the counter waiting for their morning pastries and donuts.

But there was still an undercurrent of worry down deep inside that maybe Emily had made her a co-owner earlier than planned to distract her from her grief.

No, Steph wasn't going to think that way. This had always been the plan, the two sisters working together as equals. Steph loved her job and knew she was good at it. They each had specialties—Emily was a self-taught master at cheesecakes, while Steph had learned wedding cake design that lured customers to take the twenty-minute drive from Aspen.

She turned down Third Street and swung into the alley behind the bakery, parking behind Emily's car. After leaving her SUV, she entered the vestibule with its two doors, one leading to Steph's apartment on the second floor. Emily had offered it to her when Steph hadn't felt like she could spend another moment surrounded by her memories in the rental home she'd shared with Tyler. Ever since she was a teenager, she'd occasionally lived above either the bakery or Monica's next door, and it had all been so welcome and familiar. It *should* feel like home—she spent most of her time in this building, whether upstairs or down.

The kitchen smelled wonderfully of pastry dough being transformed into croissants. Emily was there, bent over a stainless steel table, frosting cupcakes while monitoring the oven. She looked up as Steph pulled the door shut, and her smile made Steph understand the true feeling of family. Emily had strawberry blond hair she pulled into a ponytail at the back of her head, a heart-shaped face, and blue eyes that zeroed in on Steph with a startling focus.

Steph turned away to unwrap her scarf and hang up her coat on a peg next to the back door. "Hey, Em," she said over her shoulder.

"Hi, Steph," Emily said. "Everything go okay at the doctor's?"

"I'm fit as a fiddle."

Emily chuckled. "What are you—eighty? 'Fit as a fiddle'? I think the widows are rubbing off on you too much."

Steph smiled. "I know, I know."

"They roped you in way too easily to that 'Save the School-house' fundraiser."

"I don't mind keeping busy, and a historic schoolhouse is a worthy cause."

Emily let out a soft breath and put an arm around Steph's waist to give a brief squeeze. "You sure everything went okay at the doctor's? I hadn't realized Jeremy moved back home. Mrs. Thalberg told me this morning."

"Trust one of the widows to know everything."

Mrs. Thalberg, Mrs. Ludlow, and Mrs. Palmer all lived together in a remodeled Victorian house they called the Widows' Boardinghouse. They were eccentric, funny, and the elderly grandmas everyone in town seemed to need at one time or another. They also took turns working part time at Sugar and Spice Sisters.

"Was it strange having him as a doctor?" Emily asked.

Steph frowned, tension making her fingers clench hard when she reached for a clean apron. "Why would it be strange?"

Emily gave her a wide-eyed look. "Well, besides the obvious of him seeing you naked, I guess because he's a family friend. And of course, he's my hero for saving your life."

Steph's grip eased, and she finished tying the strings. She debated changing the topic, but she and her sister never kept secrets. "Actually, Doc Ericson did my physical."

Emily arched a brow. "You requested that?"

Steph turned to wash her hands at the sink before saying, "Jeremy did before I even got there."

"Ahhh."

Steph shot a look at her sister as she dried her hands. "What's that supposed to mean?"

Emily bit her lip as if in deep thought. "The expression 'ah' is one of surprise or realization."

"Realization of what?" Steph said more sharply than she'd intended to.

Emily's smile grew wider. "Isn't it intriguing that Jeremy doesn't want to be your doctor?"

"I don't think it's exactly intriguing," Steph grumbled. She logged into the computer at the corner desk where they organized the business, telling herself to focus on the day's tasks.

"Then what do you think it is?" Emily asked, her voice teasing.

Steph didn't know how to answer. She didn't know if she could talk about it yet.

"Did you talk to him to find out what's going on?" Emily continued.

"I think I'll begin with the cupcake order for the shower."

"I'm already doing that. You'll find I marked my progress on the order page."

Steph closed her eyes. Why was she feeling rattled? Emily knew her so well, knew when she was fooling herself. She swiveled her chair around to face her sister. "He said he doesn't think of me as just a friend. And he looked at me like...well, like a man hasn't looked at me in a long time." It was suddenly hard to swallow.

Emily's smile faded into concern, and she quickly sat down next to Steph and took her hand. "I shouldn't tease you. I'm sorry. Of course this must be difficult for you."

"Why? Nothing happened with Jeremy—well, I don't know what happened. We just talked. But...I felt something too, and it caught me by surprise, and I don't know how I feel about it."

Emily took her other hand too. "I think all those emotions are totally normal. And there's no rule that says you have to figure out why you feel a certain way. Recovery from losing your husband is a slow process. I don't think you should fight it or second guess yourself."

Steph knew her sister spoke from experience, that she'd suffered several miscarriages during her first marriage and had to accept that she'd never bear a child—and that her first husband had left her because of it. "But I don't know what to *do*, Em, or how I'm supposed to feel. My God, he saved my life—I should be totally grateful. And I am. But...seeing him reminds me of...that day." *And how it was all my fault that Tyler died.*

Emily's eyes glistened with obvious sympathy. "Look at it this way—is Jeremy the only person to make you remember that day?"

"Of course not. For over a year it was like I still lived there, like the shock of Tyler's absence made me experience his death over and over. It's been a little better lately."

"I'm glad to hear that. But if many things make you remember that day, is it a problem that Jeremy does, too? Maybe it's totally normal."

"I don't feel totally normal. Sometimes I think I don't remember what normal feels like."

Emily hugged her hard, enveloping her in the sweet scent of buttercream frosting. "You're creating a new normal. Be patient with yourself." She leaned back and held Steph's upper arms. "I liked Jeremy from the first time I met him. I thought it was great of him to want to move home and be our new doctor—not an easy thing to do when you've lived in Denver for most of your adult life. Maybe you're a nice connection to his old life here."

"Everything in Valentine is a connection to his old life. Besides the accident"—she was surprised to say it without a catch in her throat—"the only way he's connected to me is by memories of me trailing after him and Daniel, trying to get them to take me skiing. I was an annoying ten-year-old and they were in high school."

"He doesn't see you that way anymore." Emily patted her shoulder as she stood up and went back to her cupcakes.

Steph thought of how Jeremy had looked at her, how he'd seen her as more than someone to be pitied, someone to treat with kid gloves. Her mom acted like she couldn't even raise her voice around Steph; her dad looked at her and harrumphed, trying to hide tears. She was getting tired of everyone thinking she was fragile—or was she acting fragile? She'd tried not to.

Jeremy didn't think she was fragile; he'd asked how she was, but that hadn't stopped him from giving her a warm look that practically...smoldered.

Feeling hot with a blush, Steph put it out of her mind and went back to work.

~oOo~

After dinner that night, Steph walked a few blocks to the Silver Creek Community Center, where the widows were hosting their schoolhouse fundraiser meetings. Besides the three widows, there were usually another half-dozen locals interested in preserving the old one-room schoolhouse, including Steph's good friend Jessica Fitzjames, a reporter for the *Valentine Gazette*. Steph set a covered platter of cookies on a nearby table and then took a seat next to Jessica.

The three widows presided behind a table, looking like members of a church meeting—or the officers of the Valentine Valley Preservation Fund, which is what they were. Mrs. Thalberg was Emily's grandma-in-law, the matriarch of the Silver Creek Ranch, with box-dyed red curly hair and tasteful makeup, and the no-nonsense attitude of a rancher's wife. Mrs. Ludlow was what everyone pictured when they thought of a grandma— white-haired and slim, and she used a walker. It was hard to describe Mrs. Palmer, who wore big blond wigs and bold-patterned dresses she had sewn herself.

Tonight they were all wearing school-marm costumes. Again. They'd been wearing costumes everywhere they went for *weeks* now, promoting the upcoming fundraiser, Sleddin' Like the Oldies, for the one-room schoolhouse. They wore white blouses, long skirts, and heeled boots with buttons up the side. Steph couldn't imagine how they put those on—unless there was a hidden zipper.

They would do anything to promote their projects. The one-room schoolhouse had sat abandoned for years near the highway at the edge of Valentine Valley until the town allowed the property to be purchased for a new row of stores. Suddenly the widows of the Valentine Valley Preservation Fund, champions of historical building preservation, had realized there was a piece of history that would be torn down. When research turned up information that the children of Chinese immigrants had once been taught there, it seemed even more important that a unique part of history not be lost. But it was too late. Construction needed to begin in May, or the cost overrun penalties would cripple the construction company. Contracts had been signed.

So the widows had called their first fundraising committee meeting and announced their plan: the funds they raised wouldn't just renovate the schoolhouse into a museum; they would have to move the building to a new home. And *that* was even more expensive.

"Now that we're all together," Mrs. Thalberg said, "we'd like to introduce tonight's guest speaker."

Steph glanced at Jessica, who shrugged her shoulders as if clueless. Steph had been hoping to get more information about her committee assignment and head back to work to bake a few dozen cookies for a family reunion at the Sweetheart Inn tomorrow.

Then the door opened and in walked Jeremy Chen.

Steph straightened in her chair, shock causing her mouth to briefly sag open. He didn't see her at first, and she wanted to sink to the floor to remain unnoticed.

She realized how foolish her thoughts were; she wasn't a

coward, afraid of a man's interest—not that he'd spelled it out that directly. She could be making the whole thing up in her head.

And then he caught sight of her, and his slow smile stirred up something warm and tempting deep in her stomach, and she didn't think she was making up his interest at all.

Mrs. Thalberg gave a little clap of her hands toward Jeremy. "Dr. Chen recently moved back to Valentine Valley as our new doctor. He volunteered to join our committee—"

Steph bit back a wince.

"—because he has a special connection to the schoolhouse. Dr. Chen, would you like to explain?"

"Please call me Jeremy," he said.

"You've earned a title of importance in our community," Mrs. Ludlow pointed out, looking at him over her reading glasses.

"But it makes me sound ancient when I'm out in public, and I'm still a young guy."

The middle-aged crowd chuckled, but when Jeremy glanced pointedly at Steph again, she arched a brow.

"Mrs. Thalberg mentioned my connection to the school-house," he said, "which I only recently found out about from my dad. Our ancestors have been in Colorado since the late 1800s. They were immigrants who came to Valentine Valley to work the silver mines after constructing the Transcontinental Railroad. As you probably know from your local history, they weren't treated well."

He used his hands a bit when he talked, and pushed a lock of his dark hair out of his eyes. He seemed so at ease in front of a crowd. Of course, he'd spent years in Denver, at fast-paced hospitals for his schooling and residency. He was probably used to talking about sober topics, to providing comfort to grieving relatives, to giving good news and receiving joyful gratitude in return. He healed people, and briefly she felt amused that she only made food for a living. But she understood that making get-togethers special helped people in a different way. Still…she found herself a little intimidated in a way she hadn't this morning.

And then she remembered he hadn't been able to heal Tyler —for which she blamed herself, not him. But he still felt guilty, and that made her eyes sting. She blinked rapidly.

"Chinese immigrants usually weren't allowed in the silver mines," Jeremy continued. "Some purchased their own, because they had the patience for a certain type of mining that others refused to do. But they had to form their own communities. They weren't even allowed to set foot in Aspen. After the silver bust and the racist riots, most Chinese began to leave the Midwest, disappearing from Denver so thoroughly that people today don't even realize that there was once a Chinatown.

"But my family refused to be driven out, and they became coal miners, which lasted down through the generations until my dad decided that mining wasn't for him. You have to be wondering how this connects the Chens to the schoolhouse. As you know, that building was first used by Valentine Valley for the children of miners—white miners. But after the silver collapse, when so many people left the valley to look for work elsewhere, there weren't enough children for a school. It was taken over by my great-great-grandmother, where she taught any who wanted to learn, including immigrant children."

The committee members all looked at each other with interest, heads nodding. There was a display at the Aspen Historical Society that told the story of the Ute Native Americans displaced by the miners, but this would show a different side of their valley's history.

"Isn't this just fascinatin'?" Mrs. Palmer declared, clasping her hands together. "Anythin' else, Dr. Chen?"

"Jeremy, please," he said with a charming grin.

Mrs. Palmer fanned herself, making everyone laugh.

"I know my dad has some books my great-great-grand-mother used in her teaching. Maybe there's a diary or a journal. I'll look into it for you."

"Anything that might help raise community awareness," Mrs. Thalberg said. "It'll make people participate in the fundraiser."

"What fundraiser?" Jeremy asked.

"Stephanie explains it so much better than we can," Mrs. Ludlow said, glancing directly at her.

Every gaze turned in her direction, including Jeremy's.

"It was her idea," Mrs. Palmer added.

Jeremy crossed his arms over his chest and cocked his head, his smile expectant.

"You must have heard about Schneetag in Aspen," Steph began, "celebrating the end of the winter season."

Jeremy opened his mouth to reply, but Mrs. Palmer cut him off, "Do explain it, dear. We want him to understand."

"It's pretty simple, really," Steph continued. "You build a sled that has to make it down the hill and float across the pond at the bottom and then judges flash your score. You have a theme, do a skit, dress in costume, the works. It's a great time. We're doing the same thing as a fundraiser for the school. We're going to skip the pond and the skit. Haven't you seen our flyers?"

Everyone stared at Jeremy expectantly. Steph felt a little sorry for him.

"I must have missed them," he admitted.

The widows exchanged a look.

"Then more flyers are needed. Connie"—Mrs. Thalberg said to Mrs. Ludlow—"let's expand the social media budget to promote a few more Facebook posts. Renée," she said to Mrs. Palmer, "start planning a new TikTok video."

Mrs. Ludlow typed into her laptop at a furious pace. Mrs. Palmer bent over her phone as her fingers flew.

Jeremy's eyes widened, and when he turned to Steph, she bit her lip to keep from smiling.

"Jessica," Mrs. Thalberg called.

Jessica straightened so fast her notebook fell to the floor. "Yes, ma'am?"

"Let's run the article earlier, if possible, then schedule another closer to the event."

"I'll see what I can do," Jessica said, bending over to pick up her notebook and write, her wavy hair falling around her face.

"We're changing the Schneetag rules a bit," Steph continued. "Because the fundraiser is for a nineteenth century schoolhouse, we're going with that theme. Every sled has to be decorated as if it's straight from the Old West. Same with costumes. Every entry pays a fee, and we're going to have the spectators buy tickets to attend."

"Do you think it'll be enough?" Jeremy asked.

"I hope so," Mrs. Thalberg said. "I have some business connections to reach out to for matching funds. Moving a historical building isn't exactly cheap. The town has offered a sight at either the Rose Garden or the park on Silver Creek, so at least we don't have to purchase land. Once the move is done, we'll probably need more funds for renovation and creating the museum. But moving it is the most urgent need."

For another half hour, they discussed the more practical aspects of entry fee collection, the schedule for the big event, raffles for donated items, and the food booths. Steph took notes on her phone and tried once again to ignore the fact that this fundraiser was on a ski slope, and she hadn't skied since...

Jeremy was a good distraction. She found herself hoping he was a one-time guest instead of a regular member of the committee. Was that cowardly of her? Maybe so, but he seemed to absorb too much of her attention. Her toes tapped repetitively; her phone kept autocorrecting the wrong words when she was too flustered to spell. It would almost have been easier if his presence only brought up memories of her husband's death, but it was more than that. Emily's advice to just accept how she felt and find a new normal seemed good in the abstract, but how was she supposed to do that?

3

After the meeting, Jerry joined the small committee as they gathered around the platter of cookies Steph had brought. He watched Steph interact with the widows, "Mrs. L this" and "Mrs. P that," with a familiarity that was cute. He'd grown up being taught to appreciate his elders, but the rest of American society didn't always feel the same. Yet Steph, a woman in her twenties, saw nothing wrong with participating in a committee of mostly middle-aged and older people. And then it suddenly occurred to him—she actually *was* a widow. Was that why she was immersing herself in their causes? Was it easier to be with them than to find a new path for her life?

When Jessica excused herself to finish a story at the *Gazette*, he took the opportunity to approach Steph, who stood a little apart from the group, thoughtfully tasting one of the cookies.

"You look like you're judging your own product," Jeremy said.

Her gaze flew up to his.

"I didn't mean to startle you," he added.

She shook her head. "My own fault. I'd experimented with the cinnamon, and I'm trying to decide if it needs more."

"Can I judge, too?"

"Uh...if you want."

He reached for a cookie. "I take it from the tone of your response that you doubt my abilities as a judge."

She smiled. "No. A customer's tastes are always important. But if I changed a recipe because of every customer's suggestion, I'd have five different versions of chocolate chip cookies, five different versions of Snickerdoodles—you get the point."

"I do." He took a bite and deliberately moved the cookie around inside his mouth. "I'm tasting organic vanilla, locally sourced walnuts, free range butter. Even an aluminum cookie sheet."

Steph chuckled.

"You make a person work hard to get a laugh," he said.

"I do not." But she looked away and reached for a napkin, lips still quirking.

"I think the cookie is delicious," he said, sobering. "You're very talented."

"Stop the flattery. My sister perfected that recipe."

"Ah, so you're judging whether your sister's recipe can be improved?"

"You're really annoying."

But she was still smiling, so he wasn't dissuaded. There was more to her life than being a widow, and surely she knew that. He wanted to remind her of family, of planning for the future, rather than living in the past.

"I saw your brothers occasionally whenever I hit town," he said. "I still can't believe Daniel is all respectable now, Mr. Family Man."

"You've never come close to getting married?" she asked.

"I've thought about it, even dated a woman I thought might be the right one, until she realized I really wasn't going to live in Denver."

"Oh, that's too bad," Steph said, her smile fading.

"Yeah, well, you can't force an outsider to like a small town." The hurt was starting to fade—maybe being with Steph was encouraging that process.

"Did you consider staying in Denver for her?"

He shook his head. "I made a commitment to be here."

"You know Doc wouldn't have held you to that. We could have found another doctor."

"Not as easy as you'd think. Besides, it wasn't just Doc I was committed to. It would have been hard to explain to my mother that her son the doctor did not want to move back home."

"Ah, family obligations. They can be tricky."

"They don't seem so tricky among the Sweets. None of you left Valentine."

"Two of my brothers work on the Sweetheart Ranch, and the other in Sweet construction. Think there aren't some family obligations there?"

"And you work for your sister—I mean *with* your sister. So, yeah, we both understand family obligations." He munched a cookie and continued to eye her before swallowing. "Considering how close the Sweets are as a family, it must have been pretty strange to suddenly discover you have a big sister."

"Much worse for my dad. He had no idea his high school girlfriend was pregnant when she left town. He missed thirty years with Emily."

"That had to be tough. But you gained a sister you seem to have bonded with."

Steph smiled. "Not right away."

"Oh, that's right, I seem to remember Daniel telling me you weren't taking the news well. Something about no longer being Daddy's only little girl."

She groaned and rolled her eyes. "Unfair. I was sixteen. We're all brats at sixteen."

"But Emily won you over."

Her smile softened. "She did. She's wonderful, everything I dreamed a big sister could be. And we're friends, too, which is even better."

Jeremy wondered what Emily thought of Steph's preoccupation with the widows—but then the widows *worked* for them every day. Maybe Emily saw nothing wrong with it.

He felt his phone vibrate in his pocket and frowned. "Excuse me." He glanced at the screen. "I have to go. I'm on call."

"Thanks for sharing your family history. It makes the project even more exciting to know details of how it's connected to our past."

"I'm glad." And then he did something spontaneous—he leaned in and kissed her cheek, just a brush, really. But he could inhale her scent, something that made him think of home and baking, which shouldn't surprise him.

When he straightened, she was looking at him wide-eyed.

"Good night, Steph." He turned and left, feeling quite pleased with himself.

Steph barely resisted the urge to touch her fingers to her cheek. Now *that* was being silly. But she felt uneasy about how such a non-romantic kiss unsettled her, as if he was still in the room, focusing those dark eyes on her.

She had to admit, he was easy to talk to. He didn't have to work hard to be too funny or too kind or too...anything. Of course he was interested in her family, her business—her. But it didn't feel like simply an old family friend catching up. He'd been honest enough about the attraction which made her wonder if he was going to ask her out.

Would she say yes?

She closed her eyes and withheld a groan, turning to look out the window. She could see the Silver Creek Park in the distance, but the view didn't calm her. She wasn't going to say yes—of course not. She was a widow, which was a damned good excuse. She looked at the three elderly ladies in command of the room, then looked away. She wasn't really one of them, but she didn't feel like she was ever going to get over what had happened to her, what had happened to Tyler and her culpability in it. Jeremy would understand that.

But did she want him to be understanding?

"Stephanie?"

Steph shook herself out of her trance and turned from the window, only to see all three widows lined up before her. Steph would have stepped back from the grandmotherly onslaught, but she felt the table behind her.

"Hello, ladies," she said, far too brightly.

Had they seen Jeremy kiss her?

Mrs. Palmer and Mrs. Thalberg exchanged amused glances, while Mrs. Ludlow looked at Steph over her glasses.

"Cookie?" Steph tried to distract them by reaching quickly for the platter behind her.

"No, thank you, dear," Mrs. Thalberg said, suddenly all business. "What did you think of the presentation?"

"Uh...it was good?" she said tentatively.

"Isn't it fascinatin' how Dr. Chen's family arrived here?" Mrs. Palmer gushed. "We all have such different stories."

"I'm not sure the history of Chinese immigration to our country can be described so simply," Steph said. "Pretty sad what people will do to each other in the name of protecting what's theirs."

"Thank goodness that in the end their family prevailed and thrived," Mrs. Thalberg explained. "We can all admire that."

"We need to draw on the Chen family for the fundraiser," Mrs. Ludlow said matter-of-factly. "We'd like your help, since you and Jeremy seem to have renewed your...friendship."

Three pairs of eyes sparkled at Steph, and the few remaining committee members gave her sympathetic looks at they escaped out the door.

"My help?" Steph began. "Why wouldn't you ask Jeremy himself?"

"Dr. Chen obviously had an emergency and needed to rush off before we had the chance," Mrs. Ludlow said primly. "Why don't you visit the Chens and talk to his father? Firsthand information and historical books or papers about his ancestor will help flesh out the importance of saving the schoolhouse as we build our case for donors."

"You need to build a case, when it's so obviously a historic building that needs to be moved and preserved?"

"So you don't want to help?" Mrs. Thalberg asked.

Steph barely refrained from rolling her eyes. "I didn't say that."

Mrs. Palmer pulled her down for a hug of softness and talcum powder. "We can always count on you, Stephanie." She reached into her cleavage and pulled out an old ornate key hung on a much used strip of leather. "Just in case Mr. Chen would be interested in tourin' the schoolhouse, here's the key." She lowered her voice. "Don't tell anyone we have this. It might not be...legal." She winked.

Steph looked at the other widows, wide-eyed, but they only glanced at each other and shrugged.

"You want me to break into the schoolhouse?" Steph asked.

"It's not breaking in," Mrs. Thalberg insisted. "You have a key."

"But—"

"It will be fine, dear," Mrs. Ludlow said. "Even the new owner of the land wants us to buy the schoolhouse and take it off his hands."

Letting out a sigh, Steph put the key in her purse. Maybe the townspeople indulged the widows too much, letting them think they could get away with anything. And they always had, from chaining themselves to a historic brothel to keep it from being torn down, to leading women to throw their bras in a tree in support of a lingerie store. They liked to skirt the rules...

Steph escaped with a quick good-bye, leaving them to reach for cookies now that their work was done. As for the way they were pushing her and Jeremy together, she hadn't seen such a blatant matchmaking scheme in a long time—they must be losing their edge.

~oOo~

Late that night, Steph's nightmare returned with a vengeance. It was always the same—Tyler's avalanche beacon ringing as loud as a church bell tolling a funeral, her frantic digging, the momentary elation of discovering his body only to see Jeremy giving him CPR. The shock and pain were still so vivid; her sobs as she cradled his body ached through her chest. She woke up with a gasp, her face wet with tears.

She sat up and turned on the light, then reached for a tissue. After blowing her nose, she closed her eyes, taking deep calming breaths.

"It's just a nightmare," she told the bedraggled stuffed rabbit Hop, whom she couldn't bring herself to throw away. Tyler had won it for her at the county fair.

Perched on the chair in the corner of the room, Hop stared at her, as if silently reminding her that the nightmares were supposed to have gone away.

For a year after the accident, she'd had to tell herself not to be depressed every day. It was getting a little better now, even though there were still sudden stark moments when it seemed incomprehensible that Tyler, her high school boyfriend, the only man she'd ever loved, her husband, was dead at twenty-four.

At least her daytime tears were infrequent and manageable. Everyone had told her she'd slowly heal, that the memories would mellow, that she would think of the good times rather than the stark tragedy of his death. But no one knew the guilt she bore. She could barely face it herself. She reached for Hop and held him against her chest.

It had been months since a nightmare had disturbed her sleep. What was different?

Jeremy.

She winced and headed for the galley kitchen in her little apartment, bringing Hop with her. She stood in the dim light and sipped a glass of water, the rabbit propped on the counter.

"It's not Jeremy's fault that Tyler's death always feels so fresh," she whispered to Hop.

Jeremy was a catalyst, a reminder of the feelings she wanted to bury—the lurking fear that she hadn't been happy in her marriage. In the months before Tyler died, she'd been unsettled by a growing feeling that they'd been too young, that maybe she should have dated more before marrying her first boyfriend. After his death, her hidden doubts suddenly felt like a betrayal of the man she'd vowed to love and honor.

Her feelings of guilt rose so easily to the surface.

She picked up Hop and hugged him close. "How will I ever get past this?"

Did she even deserve to find happiness?

4

The next evening, as Jeremy was taking off his jacket and stomping the snow off his boots in the front hall, he was surprised to receive a text from Steph.

Hey Jeremy, I hope this isn't too awkward, but the widows asked me to stop by and talk to your dad. You mentioned that he had some books that might flesh out the history of the schoolhouse, and the widows are too eager to wait. Would you mind if I stop by after dinner?

Jeremy stared at the phone. He knew he should take Steph's request at face value, but he couldn't help imagining what it would be like to have a meal with her, to relax and share a conversation. Since he wasn't sure if she was ready for an actual date, his parents would make the perfect cover. He typed:

Sounds good. Can you come over right now?

There was a long pause. He was surprised to feel his stomach tense. This wasn't a big deal, he reminded himself. Just his first meal with Steph. But it felt...important.

Then a text arrived.

Sure, I'm about finished with work. Give me fifteen.

Jeremy grinned as he typed an okay and the address. She responded with:

Like I don't know where you live?

It made him feel warm with pleasure. Resisting the urge to whistle, he strolled into the kitchen, with its white cabinets and granite countertops, the large window framing the Silver Creek Park that ran behind his parents' home. The park's gazebo had practically been his sister's playhouse growing up. It was now covered in snow, the setting sun sparkling on icicles hanging from the roof.

His mom looked up from the kitchen table where she was setting out three place settings. She smiled at him, shoulder-length dark hair slightly tinged with silver strands, her glasses framing eyes shining with happiness. "Hi, Jeremy."

He wondered how he could be a little antsy living at home when it made his mother so happy?

"Hey, Mom, Steph Brissette is coming over to talk to Dad about the schoolhouse. Do you mind if she stays for dinner?"

"Of course not! Set another place at the table while I stir the Kare-kare."

His favorite Filipino stew—he loved peanut sauce. He kissed her cheek, and she cocked an eyebrow at him.

By the time the front doorbell rang, his dad had arrived home from the office, was clued in by Mom regarding their dinner guest, and was giving Jeremy the arched eyebrow that always signified amused understanding as he left the room. Jeremy only shrugged—his dad was no fool. He hoped Dad said nothing to encourage Mom, the biggest frustrated matchmaker on the planet.

Jeremy walked back to the front hall, realized he was hurrying, and had to laugh at himself. When he swung open the door, Steph stood there, wearing a short red jacket over jeans, with a knitted cap covering her blond hair.

For an extended moment, they stared at each other. Jeremy was remembering the light kiss he'd placed on her cheek, the way she'd smelled of vanilla and cinnamon. Was she thinking about it, too?

"Hi, Jeremy."

"Hey, Steph, thanks for coming."

"No, thank *you* for letting me intrude before dinner."

She gave him a lopsided, perhaps embarrassed, smile that squeezed his insides as if he was a high schooler seeing his prom date for the first time. Their gazes held another moment before she looked away with a nonchalance that didn't seem quite real.

After he invited her in and took her jacket, he saw that she was wearing a bulky white sweater that emphasized her slenderness beneath. Before he could say anything to make a fool of himself, his mom came into the living room.

"Hi, Mrs. Chen," Steph said.

"Hello, Stephanie, I'm so glad Jeremy invited you to dinner."

Steph shot him a confused look.

He shrugged. "You wanted to talk to my dad—what better time than relaxing at the kitchen table?"

She opened her mouth as if to counter, then good-naturedly let his mom draw her toward the kitchen. Jeremy followed. The sun had set behind the Elk Mountains, leaving their yard and the park glowing with snowfall. Mom had lit several candles as a centerpiece, and now moved back to the stove.

Dad stood up, setting down the phone he'd been staring at, then reached out to shake Steph's hand.

She smiled. "It's so kind of you to see me, Mr. Chen."

Dad glanced at Jeremy. "Didn't you come to see my son?"

"No!" Steph said, speaking so quickly Jeremy had to hide a chuckle.

Mom turned to Dad. "She's here about the schoolhouse rescue project."

"Oh, right," Dad said.

He gave Jeremy such an openly sympathetic look that Jeremy was starting to think dinner with his parents had been a bad idea. But after the first half hour, any awkwardness faded away as they all discussed the people they knew and loved, what his sister was up to in college in Denver, his brother's residency and training with the US Paralympic Team in Aspen. Steph talked about her brothers and sister and their families.

When Jeremy went to find the Seven Layer Bars his dad had baked last night, he heard Steph clear her throat.

"Mr. Chen, Jeremy must have told you about the fundraising efforts to move the schoolhouse and save it from demolition. He came to speak to the group about your family history."

"He did?" Dad said, turning to Jeremy.

"I thought they'd want to know more about it." Jeremy tried to sound matter of fact.

His dad nodded. "Very worthwhile. My ancestors would be happy to know their history matters, too."

Steph arched an eyebrow when Jeremy set the cookies down in front of her. "Seven Layer Bars?"

He nodded.

"We make our own version at the bakery," she said, "but it's hard to beat the original." She took a bite and closed her eyes.

Jeremy was trying to ignore the look of enjoyment on her face, her eyes closed, her brow faintly furrowed, her lips moving a bit as she tasted. He was going to have to think about something else—anything else, like reading boring bloodwork results. He saw his parents exchange an amused glance.

"Excellent," Steph said at last, opening her eyes to smile at his mother.

Mom waved a hand toward Dad. "Henry, you were judged and approved by an expert!"

Steph grinned before turning back to Dad. "We're not only

focused on fundraising, Mr. Chen. The widows are collecting information on the schoolhouse itself in anticipation of the museum. When they heard about your connection from Jeremy, they asked me to learn more. Jeremy says you have some text-books your great-grandmother used?"

Dad nodded. "I do, but before I show you those, did you know that the famous author Theodore Xu went to school there?"

Steph straightened with interest. "I recognize that name. I read one of his books in my college English elective. Are you related to him?"

"We're not," Dad said. "But he's beloved in the Chinese-American community, not to mention throughout the world, and I thought his manuscript would make the perfect center-piece of the schoolhouse museum."

"Manuscript?" Steph leaned forward, her Seven Layer Bar seemingly forgotten.

Dad smiled and lowered his voice conspiratorially. "There was a manuscript of his that was never found."

Jeremy said, "You know that's just a rumor. No one has ever found anything in writing regarding it. Xu didn't even mention the plot."

"Shh." Steph waved him off, not taking her eyes off his dad. "Go on, Mr. Chen. What have you heard?"

Jeremy leaned back in his chair, crossed his arms over his chest, and prepared to revisit the fairytale his family loved to debate.

"As Jeremy told you," Dad began, "my great-grandmother taught at the schoolhouse. In those days, with Chinese immi-grants restricted to certain jobs, children often had to work. But there was one student, Theodore Xu, who never missed school, even though it often meant he worked both before school and after. He loved books and writing more than anything, and my great-grandmother encouraged him to start work on a novel.

"When World War I interrupted, this young man felt called to represent the country his family had made their home, even though the U.S. wasn't always good to him. My great-grandmother claimed he left his unfinished manuscript with her because of his fear of riots against Chinese immigrants in Denver. But my grandparents and parents said no manuscript was ever found after her death."

"Maybe he returned for it after the war," Steph said.

Dad shook his head. "My great-grandmother swore he never returned to Valentine Valley. The memoir he wrote during his time in France became a success, not that my great-grandmother lived to see it—she never knew he became famous, which is probably the reason she never made a big deal about the manuscript. But my grandmother remembered his name, and she searched the abandoned schoolhouse years later. Nothing was found."

Steph's gaze moved from Jeremy to his parents. "But you all believe the legend."

Dad shrugged. "My great-grandmother was a no-nonsense teacher, so I don't doubt she was telling the truth. And if the manuscript had been found, wouldn't someone have produced it by now?"

"Or a homeless person used it to fuel his fire and keep warm," Jeremy pointed out.

Steph looked out the window, her blue eyes unfocused. "If we could find it, maybe it can help bring attention to the fundraiser for the schoolhouse. A world-famous author went to school there, right? His descendants would surely let us borrow it for the museum."

"Maybe," Jeremy said, "but until then, actual artifacts will have to do. Let's go find them. Mom, can we help with the dishes?"

"No, thanks, I've got your dad for that."

Steph followed Jeremy up to his bedroom, where she paused in the doorway. "If we were in high school, I'd think this was a ruse to get me alone."

He looked around at his twin bed, the small desk he'd had since kindergarten, and the bookshelf stuffed with all his favorite books over the years. "I promise not to close the door and make my parents suspicious."

She smiled as she came into the room. "You kept old family books here?"

"Not when I was a kid. Mom moved them here when she was having the living room repainted."

Nodding, she gave a sweeping glance around the small room. "Must be strange to be back in your childhood bedroom when you've lived away so long."

She walked up to the wall, where framed diplomas and certificates still hung proudly, as if his mom had to document his life.

"It's temporary," he said. "I already bought a house a couple blocks away. Just waiting for the closing to be scheduled. Where are you living?"

"In the apartment above the bakery. I—we—had only been renting a house...before."

She kept looking at photos on the wall, so he couldn't see her expression. Packing up her marriage and its memories at such a young age had to have been hard.

But he sensed she didn't want to talk about it, and who could blame her? He went to his bookshelf, looking for his grand-mother's books, then said over his shoulder, "Does your mom still keep your bedroom like you left it?"

"Yep. It's like a part of my life in snapshot form."

He chuckled, then found what he was looking for and sat down on the bed. He thought she'd pull up the chair, but instead she sat beside him as he opened the Old Farmer's Almanac of 1911. As they paged through, they took turns pointing out notes scribbled in the margin in Chinese characters, which neither of them could read.

"Probably teacher notes," Jeremy said. "I can have my mom look at it—she's still fluent."

"She came from the Philippines, right?"

He nodded. "There's a large Chinese community there. She met my dad when she was a TA for a college Mandarin course he was taking in Denver. He doesn't remember much of the language at all."

"I'm glad I'm not the only one who can't remember a language I took in school."

He turned his head to smile and realized how close she really was. He would only have to slide over an inch, and he'd be touching her. A lock of her hair dropped forward, brushing her cheek, and he almost tucked it behind her ear. When their eyes met, she quickly focused back on the almanac.

"You said there are other books?" she asked.

Did she sound a little breathless? Was she feeling everything he was feeling?

If so, she was obviously trying to ignore it, so he would remain patient. He showed her a math textbook, and another about plant life in Colorado. They scanned through them but there were only more scattered notes in Chinese. It was hard to concentrate, when already his patience was deserting him. All he could think about was when and how to ask her out. He'd just made the decision to ask when his mom appeared in the open doorway. To his surprise, Steph didn't jump off the bed.

"Jeremy," Mom said, "ever since the schoolhouse fundraiser began, I've been looking through old boxes in the attic. I came across your great-great-grandmother's journal yesterday. It's mostly lesson plans written in Chinese, from the little I've read. I didn't see any mention of her famous student, but I can read it again."

"Thanks, Mrs. Chen," Steph said, getting to her feet. She turned back to Jeremy. "Let's keep the manuscript quiet, okay? We don't want break-ins at the schoolhouse. I'll discuss it with the widows and see how they want to handle it."

Silently cursing his timing, Jeremy followed Steph and his mom downstairs, where Steph went right to the front door. He retrieved her coat for her.

She smiled as she slid her arms in and zipped the front. "Thanks for your help, Jeremy. And you, too, Mrs. Chen, especially for the delicious dinner. Please thank your husband for me."

And then she sailed out the door, leaving Jeremy shaking his head at the missed opportunity.

~oOo~

Steph got into her frigid car, started it up, then sat for a moment, hands on the wheel, eyes closed.

She'd only just escaped in time.

What had she been thinking, sitting on his bed, so close she could hear him breathing and feel the warmth of his arm as it sometimes brushed hers?

She'd been thinking of the books as a window on the past, and her interest in the history, and wanting to see everything at the same time he did.

And instead, she'd barely been able to concentrate on anything except wondering if he'd try to kiss her. She'd already told herself she wasn't ready to date, but was her mind—her body—trying to tell her something else?

5

Later that night, Jeremy leaned against the edge of the pool table in the back room of Tony's Tavern and watched Daniel Sweet sink a ball in the nearest pocket. Daniel straightened, crossed his tattooed arms over his chest, and donned a satisfied grin.

"Yeah, yeah," Jeremy grumbled. "Finish the game—you know you will. I'll get us another beer."

He saw Tony's son Ethan, working a shift in between college semesters, deliver drinks at another table. Jeremy held up his empty mug, and Ethan nodded, smiling, as he passed.

Daniel finished off the last two balls and sat back down at their table, wearing a satisfied grin. "I'm a father of four now, and I still have it."

"Not sure when you find the time to practice."

"I don't. I'm naturally gifted."

Jeremy rolled his eyes. As the beers arrived and Daniel asked Ethan about college, Jeremy found himself glancing around the back room, filled with people he'd grown up with as well as new arrivals to Valentine Valley. They'd been incredibly welcoming when he became the town's new doctor, dropping off coffeecake at his parents', inviting him for a round of golf. Doc himself looked so rested and was taking ski trips right and left. There was no doubt that Jeremy was needed—which made guilt gnaw at him over his conflicting feelings about being in Valentine.

Then his brother Eric limped into the back room. Several hellos echoed from group to group, and someone made a comment on Eric's latest training sessions. Jeremy watched with pride as his brother moved through the crowd, so at ease with everyone, so accomplished, although once Eric had thought his dreams destroyed forever by the car accident that had taken his leg.

Eric sat down opposite Jeremy, then glanced at the pool table. "Did

Daniel win again?"

"Daniel did," Daniel said.

"Guess you have a new purpose now, Jeremy—getting better than Daniel. Surely you have the time to practice. Or does doctoring keep you too busy?" Eric chuckled, knowing the answer. "Of course, you must really be desperate for something to do if you've taken up with the widows' latest scheme."

"I'm only helping out," Jeremy said. "After all, we have a family connection to the schoolhouse."

Daniel arched an eyebrow as he regarded Jeremy. "My sister's involved in the schoolhouse project."

"I know," Jeremy said, then hesitated, lowering his voice. "How's she doing?"

Daniel's broad grin faded to a rueful smile. "She's doing good—as good as can be expected."

"She hasn't skied since Tyler died," Eric said.

"She hasn't?" Jeremy asked Daniel.

Daniel shook his head. "She's not ready. And we're not pushing her. None of us know what it feels like to be swept away by an avalanche and lose your husband because of it."

They all nodded in silence for a moment. Jeremy remembered Tyler's bright smile, and the love in his eyes when he looked at Steph.

"Did she get some counseling?" Jeremy asked.

"She did," Daniel answered. "And she says it helped her with the PTSD. Time helped, too—it's almost been a year and a half."

"Is she dating anyone?" Jeremy regretted the question the moment it came out of his mouth.

Both men turned as one to stare at him. He let the question stand without any more explanation—what was the point?

"No." Daniel's seriousness morphed into a slow smile.

Jeremy was relieved. Some part of him worried that his good friend might object to Jeremy pursuing his sister.

Daniel continued, "Are you having thoughts in that direction?"

"Maybe. But how does a person get over the past? How can she ever forget that I couldn't save Tyler?"

"She knows you did everything you could," Eric said, briefly putting his hand on Jeremy's forearm.

"Logically, sure," Jeremy said. "But emotionally? In her heart? I don't know..."

Just then, Steph walked into the back room with Jessica. She was smiling and happy, calling for a beer from Ethan, teasing Whitney Thalberg about a new lingerie display in the front window of her store, Leather and Lace. More than one person gave Steph a sad look behind her back, and Jeremy found himself resenting their pity, which she could probably feel. She wasn't a victim, but a strong woman who was moving ahead with her life. He admired the hell out of her.

Steph smiled when she saw Daniel and headed toward their table. With a wave, Jessica continued on to other friends. Daniel stood to give his sister a hug.

"You're my one brother who doesn't smell like cows," Steph said.

Daniel laughed. "Yeah, but occasionally it's sawdust or grease in the construction business. My wife says it turns her on."

Everyone groaned.

"Look at you two hugging," Jeremy said. "I remember you locked horns when you were kids."

"That was a long time ago." Daniel grabbed an extra chair for Steph.

"And I seem to remember you weren't that fond of me either," Steph teased Jeremy as she sat down.

Wide-eyed, Jeremy put a hand on his chest. "Me? You were only Daniel's kid sister. I barely paid any attention to you."

"I guess she always wished you would," Daniel said.

Everyone laughed, Steph's cheeks flushed, but at least she was smiling, too.

"I wanted to be one of the boys," she said, "no surprise there."

"And we didn't make any time for you," Jeremy said. "Not very nice of us."

Eric leaned toward Steph. "I was in the same boat, the kid brother trying to hang out."

"You and I probably have a lot to talk about," Steph said.

And Jeremy felt a stab of something he refused to label as jealousy.

Daniel clapped Eric on the shoulder. "The dartboard is open. Are you ready?"

"Are *you* ready to be crushed?" Eric retorted.

The two stood up, picked up their beers, and left.

Steph and Jeremy turned to look at each other.

"Subtle," she said.

He chuckled. "I don't think I'm very good at hiding my thoughts from my brother."

There was a silence that lingered a little too long, and he held his breath. Would she laugh it off? Leave?

Ethan arrived with Steph's beer, and after she took her first sip, she seemed to forget what he'd said.

"So," she began, leaning her elbows on the table as she looked at him, "I'm curious why you didn't tell your parents that you'd gotten involved in the schoolhouse project."

"You know, I'm not sure." Their conversation felt strangely intimate in a packed, loud bar. "I could say it was because I was so busy at work that I forgot about it, but that wouldn't be true."

"Which isn't true, that you're busy or that you forgot?" she teased.

He gave her a rueful grin. "Maybe both."

"Most people would be happy not to be too busy at work."

"That's true. And the relaxed pace is certainly better than an ER in Denver."

"But...?"

"I think I haven't talked to my parents about things because I might let slip my ambivalence about being in Valentine Valley. I don't want to hurt their feelings if I end up moving back to Denver."

She sat back in her chair, eyebrows raised. "Really?"

He quickly added, "I wouldn't leave unless I had a replacement lined up."

She waved a hand. "I know you wouldn't abandon patients. I just didn't realize you were so unhappy here."

"I'm not. Really. But I never gave myself the chance to explore different options. Maybe I should have lived in the city a few more years post-residency. Maybe I took the wrong path." He suddenly realized he hadn't spoke about this to anyone, not even his brother. And here he was confiding in Steph so easily.

She nodded and took another sip of her beer pensively, her gaze unfocused. "I worry that I made some wrong decisions." Then she seemed to catch herself and gave him a too bright smile. "I guess it's part of the human condition."

When she began to stand up, he touched her hand. "What wrong decisions?"

She sank back down on the edge of the chair. "Are you on the clock, Doc?"

"You know I'm asking as your friend," he gently chided.

She nodded with a sigh. "I know. And if I feel like I can talk about it, I'll remember you asked." She stood up, wearing a more natural smile even as she slid her hand from beneath his. "The pool table is open."

"Are you challenging me?"

"Prepare to lose your shirt."

~oOo~

The next day at work, Steph thought about her evening spent with Jeremy at his home and then at Tony's Tavern. She'd felt in turns awkward and interested, excited and nervous. He had a way about him that made her laugh even as he made her feel desirable. Already, her determination to say no if he asked her on a date was slipping away.

Nothing like a visit to the widows to make her stop thinking romantic thoughts. When she'd called before dropping by, they'd insisted she have dinner with them—she'd long ago given up her annoyed thoughts that everyone seemed to want to feed her out of pity. People wanted to help, and there was little else they could do. She was the one who'd had to figure out how to live with her grief and guilt.

The Widows' Boardinghouse was a beautiful Victorian home on the outskirts of the Silver Creek Ranch. The wraparound porch always made Steph want to curl up there with a good book on a summer evening. She drove around back to the entrance near the kitchen, the room where every visitor was made to feel at home.

Mrs. Thalberg answered the door, wearing a big smile, her nineteenth-century bonnet hanging down her back, the ribbons tangled together at her neck. Her long skirt looked fuller today, probably with a petticoat or two underneath.

"Steph, so good to see you!"

She kissed Mrs. Thalberg's perfumed cheek. "Thanks for having me."

Soon Steph was sitting in the cow-themed kitchen with the three ladies still in their prairie schoolteacher wardrobes, while Mrs. Palmer told her about researching nineteenth-century dress patterns to sew, Mrs. Thalberg served chili and cornbread, and Mrs. Ludlow pressed her about her visit to the Chens.

"Let the girl eat, Connie," Mrs. Thalberg admonished.

Mrs. Ludlow frowned at her friend over her glasses. "Are we to eat in silence?"

Steph swallowed a bit of cornbread, then smiled. "It's fine. I can certainly talk—it might slow me down from eating too fast."

"Don't you get enough to eat, darlin'?" Mrs. Palmer asked with concern.

Steph gave an inward sigh. "Of course I do. I was making a joke. I not only bake—I cook."

"All by yourself?" Mrs. Palmer continued.

"I'm fine by myself. When I want family around me, I go to my parents'. I work with my sister and you ladies and wait on customers all day. Believe me, a quiet dinner is sometimes nice."

"We're overbearing," Mrs. Thalberg said, exchanging a knowing look with Mrs. Ludlow.

Steph threw her hands wide. "You are not! Let's discuss the Chens. I had dinner with them last night."

The ladies all leaned forward eagerly while she told them what Mr. Chen had said about the schoolbooks with Chinese writing in the margins.

"But the best part is that there's a mystery that might solve all our fundraising problems."

"A mystery?" Mrs. Ludlow echoed, brows knitting in concentration.

"Do you know the writer Theodore Xu?"

"I have all of his books," Mrs. Thalberg said. "Did you know he was from the Roaring Fork Valley?"

"Well, there's more," Steph said. "Apparently he was educated in our very own schoolhouse."

"I should have realized that," Mrs. Ludlow, the retired teacher, murmured. "I didn't think he lived in Valentine."

"Before he went to fight in France during World War I, he left behind a manuscript he'd been writing. Jeremy's great-great-grandmother, who taught Mr. Xu, promised to keep it for him. But no one knows what happened to it."

All the widows leaned forward.

Steph briefly held her breath, wondering if Mrs. Palmer's big blond wig might topple off. It did not. "I believe no one but the Chen descendants know about the manuscript. Jeremy's great-great-grandmother didn't even realize how famous he would get. She might have misplaced or destroyed it. Or hidden it very, very well."

The widows looked at each other, giving off a vibe of silent communication. It was as if after being friends their entire lives, they could read each other's minds.

"It could still be there," Mrs. Thalberg mused, chin resting on her hand. "If no one knew about it, no one would have searched. The place has been locked up for decades."

"You still have that key I gave you?" Mrs. Palmer asked.

"Of course," Steph said.

"Then you should go look for the manuscript."

Steph straightened, dropping her spoonful of chili back into the bowl. "What?"

"That is a good idea," Mrs. Ludlow said calmly. "We don't want word of this to get out. It could start a frenzy of trespassers from all over the world."

"Won't *I* be trespassing?" Steph asked with faint sarcasm.

"I gave you the key!" Mrs. Palmer said. "And take that nice Dr. Chen."

Steph felt her face heat and hoped they'd think it was the spicy chili. "Why Jeremy? The three of you could come with me."

"Nonsense," said Mrs. Ludlow. "It's Jeremy's family history. He should be there. And my walker would get in the way. We widows go together or not at all."

They were actually sharing a smile of triumph that they'd made it hard for her to refuse. She wasn't beaten yet.

"Jeremy isn't related to the author," Steph pointed out.

"Why wouldn't you want his help?" Mrs. Thalberg asked.

They seemed genuinely interested—too interested. How was Steph to give a good answer without revealing her own conflicted feelings and diving into old wounds she didn't want to revisit?

Then she remembered playfully beating Jeremy at pool, leaning side by side on the edge of the table as they talked, feeling alternately like a high school girl with a crush, and a woman who wanted more.

"I just don't want to inconvenience him," she finished, knowing it sounded lame.

"Nonsense," Mrs. Ludlow said briskly. "Being a doctor in Valentine Valley gives him much more free time than in Denver."

And he wasn't happy about it, Steph thought. Maybe he needed a diversion. "All right, I'll ask him."

"Good!" Mrs. Palmer clapped her hands together.

It would sound like she was asking him on a date, Steph realized, and inwardly winced. Hadn't she been the one resisting dating?

6

Three days later, on a Saturday morning, Jeremy pulled up in a parking spot on Main Street, near Sugar and Spice Sisters. The sun was already cresting the Sawatch Range, the sky so blue and clear it seemed unreal. As he got out of his pickup truck, he inhaled the crisp, cold air and felt the promise of a good day—Steph had asked him out.

Not that he was going to tease her about it; he knew she was determined that searching an abandoned, dusty schoolhouse was not a real date. When she'd texted him, although he couldn't hear her voice, he thought the tone seemed a little stilted, just the barest facts about the widows wanting his help.

Not Steph, but the widows. She was emphatic about that. Was she trying to emphasize she didn't consider herself one of them? He hoped so.

Once on the sidewalk, Jeremy paused outside the plate glass windows on either side of the bakery door. One side was a literal waterfall of cookies on display. The other side showcased only a wedding cake, with tiers of white-frosted layers decorated with another waterfall, this time of delicate flowers made of frosting flowing down the side.

And he had a sudden memory of Cassie, who wanted to marry him but couldn't bear to leave Denver. And he hadn't been able to stay. Their inability to find a compromise used to haunt him, but the hurt had faded. The memories were sepia-colored now, so far in the past it seemed like ancient history.

Was that why he felt so disconnected from Valentine Valley? Was there some part of him that wanted to reconnect with Cassie, to make a different choice a year ago? But he couldn't bring back that past, couldn't change the person he'd become when he made the decision to honor his commitment to this town.

And when he saw Steph behind the glass display case inside, waiting on a customer, short blond ponytail bobbing at the back of her head, her smile so wide and full of pleasure, he suddenly knew that Cassie really *was* in his past, that it was time to give Valentine Valley the chance it deserved.

To give his interest in Steph a chance to grow into something more.

Jeremy opened the door and stepped inside to be enfolded in the warm smell of cinnamon. On the left was a glass display case full of mouthwatering goodies. In the back, next to a swinging door was tall cooler full of cheesecakes. On the right near a display of coffee carafes were scattered chairs and tables, decorated with red lanterns and little dragons—he didn't remember the last time he'd seen Lunar New Year's decorations in a non-Chinese business. He was impressed.

Steph gave him a nod, and he couldn't quite read her emotions. He didn't mind—there was plenty of time. Since she was busy, he ordered a cookie loaded with chocolate chunks from Mrs. Palmer, who wore a bakery apron with CAN I FROST YOUR COOKIES over her gingham prairie dress. Jeremy coughed to hide his chuckle. Prominently displayed on top of the display case was a cardboard replica of the schoolhouse, with a slot for donations. He put some money in.

Mrs. Palmer winked at him as she handed over the cookie and an empty cup for his coffee. "Thanks for your help, Doc."

"Any time."

It felt a little strange to be called "Doc" by someone old enough to be his grandmother. But he liked it.

After filling his cup at the coffee station, he took a seat in the corner where he could watch Steph work. She moved among her customers with ease, her smile bright, her attention focused. He could see that she and her sister took great pride in feeding the community, making their holidays and weddings even more special. Steph and Emily talked to each other with animation, with love, and he remembered that their relationship had blossomed with hard work. And then Emily glanced at him and whispered something to Steph, who blushed.

Jeremy could hear snatches of their conversation, especially Steph saying, "I need to finish...he doesn't mind waiting..."

And he didn't. He was pleasantly surprised to find that he could eat his delicious cookie, sip his coffee, and just watch the citizens of Valentine Valley come to satisfy their sweet tooths. Nobody was in a rush; everyone was smiling and seemed to know everyone else. Maybe the slower pace of smalltown life was coming back to him.

A thin, middle-aged woman who looked vaguely familiar came through the front door, holding the hand of a toddler, perhaps three years old, whose dark hair sprouted in three uneven pigtails from her head.

"Mommy!" the toddler called, then ran behind the display counter.

Emily picked her up to bestow a hug and kiss. "Avery, sweetie, I missed you!"

Avery lay her head on her mom's shoulder and snuggled in

with obvious contentment. Steph watched them, smiling, before she turned back to her customer.

Emily glanced at the woman who'd brought her daughter. "Wendy, how'd it go today?"

Wendy. Now Jeremy remembered why he knew her. Wendy Brissette, Steph's mother-in-law.

"Fine as always," Wendy said. "Your daughter brightens every moment we're together."

"You know how much I appreciate your help," Emily said.

Wendy waved a hand dismissively. As they discussed what Avery had been up to the last few hours, and Avery munched on a cookie, Steph came over to Jeremy. He stood up.

She saw where his gaze was focused, and her smile faded a bit. "You remember my mother-in-law?"

He nodded, then asked quietly, "How's she doing?"

"Okay. She still has Tyler's brother, Cody. She watches Avery part-time each week. I think caring for a toddler became sort of a lifeline for her."

Jeremy shook his head in sadness.

Wendy casually glanced over her shoulder at them, then her stare turned focused and unreadable.

Jeremy sighed. "I'm sure I won't be her favorite person."

"Don't think about it that way. No one blames you for Tyler's death."

"No?" he asked, studying her.

She didn't even hesitate as she shook her head. "No one."

Relief washed over him like a warm tide.

Steph couldn't miss the sorrow and guilt that flickered in Jeremy's eyes. She'd been so focused on herself, and how it felt to regularly see the man who'd saved her life, that she'd never imagined how *he* must feel, as the doctor who couldn't save Tyler. Did he blame himself? She hoped she hadn't made him feel that way. And she didn't want him to worry about Wendy either.

Steph took his arm and pulled him toward the counter. "Wendy, you remember my friend Jeremy Chen, don't you?"

Wendy's expression remained unchanged. "I do."

Gone was the longing gaze full of love that Wendy usually gave Steph, the one that made her feel needed, but also sad and a little overwhelmed. She never questioned those feelings closely—thinking about anything regarding Tyler had been too painful.

"Jeremy's back in town to be our new doctor," Steph continued, hearing herself sound too cheerful, but unable to find a way to stop.

Both Jeremy and Wendy were looking at her curiously.

It occurred to Steph that if—*when* she started dating again, Wendy would know she'd moved on from her grief. Could Wendy, as a mom, ever do that? Would Wendy think Steph would leave her Brissette family behind? Wendy was a second mother to her—that would never change. Steph would find a way to make sure Wendy and Cody knew they would always be family to her.

But right now, Wendy was looking at Jeremy as if he was a bug on the floor. Steph felt paralyzed with indecision. How did she smooth this over without revealing things she might not want to reveal?

"Aunt Steph!"

That little voice jarred her out of her thoughts, and she bent to sweep Avery into her arms.

"I rode Daddy's horse," Avery said, her dark eyes wide with excitement.

"All by yourself?" Steph asked.

Wendy's expression relaxed into a smile. "She was lucky

enough to ride with her daddy. She was way up on the horse when I picked her up earlier today."

"Wow," Steph said. "Did you hear that, Jeremy?"

Drawn into the conversation, Jeremy said, "That is the best. I've never been riding before, so you beat me to it."

Steph stared at him. "You've never ridden a horse?"

"Never." He acted as if he was going to say something, then changed his mind. "Avery, you're such a big girl."

"I know," she said solemnly.

Steph and Jeremy exchanged a smile.

Wendy's pleasant expression faded as she looked at the two of them.

Steph felt again that clutch of pain, as if she'd disappointed her mother-in-law. Was she ready to feel like this?

After the last customer left by the front door, Emily joined the circle around her daughter.

"Jeremy," Emily said, "Steph's been telling me about the schoolhouse, and how your family is related to one of the original teachers. It's so wonderful that you're helping to bring to life the history of the Chinese in Valentine Valley." She glanced at her daughter, her brow furrowing. "We adopted Avery from China, and it's so important to us that she understands her culture."

"Has she been to the Lunar New Year celebrations in Denver?" Jeremy asked. "They have lion dancers and dragons."

"We've heard about it," Emily said, "but didn't think she was old enough to enjoy it last year."

"I'd be happy to escort the whole family," Jeremy said. "I'm sure Aunt Steph would be fascinated."

Emily bit her lip to hide a smile, Steph blushed, and Wendy folded her arms across her chest.

"We'll give that some thought," Emily said. "Right now, we're focused on designing our sled—"

"By 'we' she means the Fantastic Four," Steph interrupted.

Jeremy arched a brow.

"Stop calling us that," Emily said, laughing. "I think you know my friends, Jeremy, at least by their maiden names: Brooke Thalberg, Monica Shaw, and Whitney Winslow. We invited Steph to join us, but she's building a sled with our brothers, right? Shouldn't I be upset I wasn't invited?"

"Of course you were invited," Steph said, leaning her shoulder into her sister. "But we all knew that the four of you would group together."

"Huh," Emily said.

Avery arched away from Steph, knowing her mom would catch her. Steph laughed and tried to keep her, nibbling her neck, inducing cute baby chuckles, before letting her go.

Wendy's expression softened, and to Steph's surprise, so did Jeremy's. He must be a guy who liked kids, since he was a family practitioner.

"Steph, whenever you're ready to go, I'd be happy to drive," Jeremy said.

And Wendy frosted right back up again.

Steph hurriedly said to her mother-in-law, "The widows asked us for help with the schoolhouse."

"Then don't let me keep you," Wendy said. She said good-bye to Emily, gave Avery a little tickle under the chin, and left.

As Jeremy stepped away to dispose of his cup and napkin, Emily gently elbowed Steph and murmured, "Don't worry about Wendy. It'll just take time."

Once Steph and Jeremy were in his car, he didn't mention Wendy, and Steph was relieved. Though it was less than two miles to the schoolhouse out near Rt. 82, Jeremy asked about Emily's little girl, and Steph told him about her first marriage, the miscarriages that caused her husband to end it, and how long Emily and Nate had worked on the adoption process.

"They're so happy now," Steph said.

"It's obvious. And although Emily seems worried, I'm sure she'll do a great job helping Avery to enjoy all of her heritage."

Steph nodded, grateful that he understood.

They drove toward the schoolhouse, a solitary, weathered clapboard building with a belfry where a bell must have once rung. It was situated on the highway that ran down valley, once central enough that all the children could walk or ride there. Steph thought about what it must have been like for the immigrant children to have their own schoolhouse, when they hadn't been welcome other places. This building had once been the place that tried to help them find a better life.

It had certainly helped the author, Theodore Xu.

Jeremy parked on the road in front of the schoolhouse, because the small parking lot beside it was unplowed. A shovel had been left beside the steps, which were still piled with snow.

Steph fished for the large, old-fashioned key in her purse and held it up. "I really know how to show a guy a good time."

"So you're admitting you asked me on a date."

Shocked, she swiveled her head toward him, only to find him wearing a teasing smile.

She let out her breath in a laugh. "Very funny."

"Not so funny. I'm alone with you, rather than in a crowded bar. That makes it a pretty good date."

"How about if we concentrate on why we're here," she said, removing her winter gloves and pulling on her work gloves.

"For now. And in the spirit of why we're here, my mom told me she read through my great-great-grandmother's journal, and didn't find anything about a hidden manuscript, not even a mysterious clue."

"I didn't think we'd be that lucky. Let's shovel our way to the door and see what we find."

After they stepped out of the car, Jeremy slung a backpack

over his shoulder, squinting at the schoolhouse against the sunlit blue sky. "Were we supposed to ask permission of someone before going in?"

She held up the key again. "Freely given to me by the widows."

"The widows aren't the owners."

"True. But imagine the publicity this could generate."

He grinned. "So we're living life dangerously."

She just blinked at him, surprised by how much she liked seeing him wearing a conspiratorial smile. She looked back at the schoolhouse and spoke over her shoulder. "If you can call a doctor and a pastry chef rebels. And besides, the owners *want* us to succeed in moving the schoolhouse. They don't want to tear it down."

"Then let's do this." Jeremy started removing the straps that held a ladder to the roof rack of his car.

Steph grabbed the shovel, cleared a narrow path up the front stairs, then put the key in the lock. It rotated easily, silently, as if recently oiled. She turned the big brass knob and pushed. Cold stale air wafted toward her, smelling of old wood and disuse. Instead of entering into the main schoolroom, she was in a small cloakroom lined with broken metal coat pegs jutting from the wall, cobwebs stretched between them.

"Watch where you're stepping," Jeremy called, "in case there are holes in the floor."

There weren't holes, but there were scattered pieces of wood and metal brackets, as if from broken desks. The windows at either end of the vestibule were boarded up at the bottom, but the top let in faint light behind tattered curtains.

Steph stepped carefully toward the interior door, which led into the main schoolroom. The plaster walls were damaged in places, showing broken strips of lath. Piles of wood might once have been student benches or desks. Old candles perched on debris, and discarded clothes or blankets overflowed one corner. A slate platform that had probably been used for a wood or coal stove had been constructed against the back wall, the broken pipe vent dangling from the ceiling above. She wished a stove still existed—it was pretty cold.

"Do you think there's an attic, or only some storage up there?" Steph asked, hands on her hips as she peered up into the vent hole.

Jeremy propped the ladder against the wall. "More places to search, I guess. I can't believe a manuscript would be lying around like garbage."

"It probably would have been burned for fuel long ago," she reminded him.

"Maybe, but let's see what we can find."

To Steph's surprise, he swung his backpack to the floor and pulled out water bottles and leather work gloves. He rooted around in the depths so long she leaned over to look.

"Uh uh uh," he said, pulling the backpack away.

"Your work supplies are a secret?"

"Who says it's work supplies?"

He again gave her that grin that felt both cute and naughty, warming her skin.

"I probably shouldn't have come so prepared, since it's your date." He rose to his feet.

"It's not my date." She felt herself blushing again—she hadn't blushed so much in years!

"Would it be so bad to date me?" he asked quietly, his smile growing rueful. "I know things were uncomfortable with your mother-in-law. Does that mean you're not ready?"

"I don't know how I feel." She crossed her arms over her chest, telling herself it was only the cold that made her want to huddle into herself.

"I can't claim to know all my feelings either, but I knew I

didn't want to be your doctor, and in examining that, I realized I was thinking about you a lot, even more so now that we've been thrown together." He took a step closer to her.

Her heart was suddenly beating much too fast as she looked up at him.

"I'll back off if you want me to," he said softly, then cupped her cheek.

Her skin was cold, but his hand felt so warm, and she didn't turn away when he lowered his head to kiss her. His lips were gentle on hers, testing, exploring. And then she let herself lean against his chest.

The kiss changed then, became deeper, and she met it with a rush of passion. Their arms went around each other, her head pressed to his shoulder. She forgot where she was, she forgot who she was, except a woman who'd missed intimacy and closeness.

She suddenly pressed her hands against his chest, breaking the kiss.

He looked down at her, dark eyes heavy with passion. "I didn't plan to do that."

"I know," she whispered. She disentangled herself from his embrace. "And it's not like I'm upset. I—I don't know what I am."

"And you don't have to know right now. We have plenty of time."

"Let's just search the schoolhouse."

"Okay." He picked up the work gloves that had dropped to the floor and handed them to her.

"Thanks. You want to start to the right and I'll go left?"

"Sure."

She thought that would keep him away from her while she settled herself, but it didn't work. She was very aware of him being only a few feet away from her. She tried not to look at his back when he couldn't see her, the width of his shoulders, the way his fleece jacket stretched when he moved.

At least her embarrassment was keeping her warm, even as she could practically see her breath.

After finishing their search of the main school room, Jeremy set up the ladder in the cloak room so that Steph could climb up and see the attic storage. She shined a flashlight into the darkness while he steadied the ladder. There were more crates and boxes scattered across the floor in various states. She thought something skittered away in the far corner.

"Ugh," she said, "it looks like we'll have to explore."

"I came prepared. I have some camp lanterns in the car. Come on down, and I'll go get them."

As she descended the ladder, landing close to him, she tried to focus on their task rather than how much she liked being near him.

"I'm impressed by your thorough preparations," she said.

"Perhaps before we get filthy exploring the attic, we should take a break for a picnic."

"A picnic?" she echoed, bemused.

"I'm as prepared as a Boy Scout."

She chuckled. "I could take that too many ways."

As she turned away, he leaned close and spoke softly next to her ear. "Please do."

She pretended not to understand what he meant.

Jeremy knew she understood as he watched the back of her neck redden. But he didn't push the issue—he wanted flirtation to remind her that they could have fun together. Instead, he cleared a large spot on the floor, then spread a light blanket out. Steph watched, arms crossed beneath her breasts, her smile bemused.

He brought out a selection of small sandwiches, a container of berries, and another of nuts. He did not dream of giving a pastry chef any kind of baked goods, so he'd brought some specialty candies from Just Desserts. Last was a bottle of wine and two plastic goblets.

"My, my, you thought of everything," Steph murmured.

After taking off her boots, she sat down cross-legged on the blanket, and Jeremy joined her. They filled their paper plates and began to munch.

"I'm surprised how hungry aimless searching can make me," she said between bites. "This is very good, thanks."

"I made them myself. A busy guy who lives on his own gets good at the basics."

"I think there's flavored cream cheese on this ham sandwich."

"I never reveal my secrets, just like a good pastry chef."

Laughing, she covered her mouth with her napkin.

"If you don't mind a more serious topic, how's your mother-in-law doing? Does she have a husband to lean on?"

Steph's smile faded, but her brow furrowed with contemplation, rather than offense. Jeremy let his breath out slowly in relief.

"No, her husband ran out on her and their two sons when the boys were little."

He winced. "How terrible. I'm so sorry to hear that. It must have made her even closer to her sons."

"She always has been. Tyler adored his mother."

To Jeremy's relief, she spoke her husband's name quite matter-of-factly.

Steph continued, "She worked two jobs throughout their childhood to make ends meet. When her older son got into trouble and had to spend a year in jail, she was there to welcome him home and help him create a new life. She extended that welcome to me, since I started dating Tyler when we were only sixteen. His death made us even closer in grief, and more than once she's said how grateful she is that our relationship hasn't changed."

When she frowned, Jeremy knew she was remembering Wendy's behavior at Sugar and Spice Sisters.

"Perhaps it helps her feel close to her son's memory when she's with you," he said, "and maybe the realization that things might not stay the same is finally hitting her—not that she'd ever lose your love."

Steph's lips turned up in a wry smile. "I know things won't remain frozen as they are. I think she knows it, too. We just have to be a little patient while she figures it out."

We.

What did that mean? Was Steph including him or did she mean herself and her family? Well, Jeremy knew how to be patient, too, when he wanted something important. And he wanted Steph.

"Thanks for the meal, Jeremy." She dabbed a napkin to her mouth. "Ready to keep working?"

He nodded, and together they packed away their picnic lunch. He grabbed the camp lanterns and two headlamps from the car, and soon the two of them were exploring the attic, laughing as they pulled off cobwebs or accidentally zapped each other in the eyes with a headlamp beam. When they'd explored every piece of broken crate or desk, they exchanged a confused glance.

"Where else could a manuscript be hidden?" Steph asked, hands on her hips.

She looked captivating with her smudged face and a lock of hair falling into her eyes, but Jeremy didn't say that aloud.

"Outside?" he said. "I don't believe there was a cellar, but if there was one, it might have an outside entrance."

She wrinkled her nose. "That's a lot of digging through snow. And the conditions are probably bad for a paper manuscript. Can you think of anywhere inside we might have missed?"

They each turned a slow circle. Then Jeremy walked to where the sloping roof met the half wall. There was no plaster on the walls, just regularly spaced wooden studs. Kneeling down, he peered past the edge of the attic floor.

"There's a gap here where the floor meets the studs," he said.

Steph joined him, leaning forward until her head brushed the cold wall. "It's the perfect width. But doesn't this opening go all the way down to the first floor?"

He found a metal hinge and dropped it down the opening. It dinged side to side during the descent before it thumped somewhere down below.

"Hiding a manuscript down here would make it really hard to retrieve it," he said. "You'd have to tear out the walls in the schoolroom."

"Unless..." Steph began, her smile slowly growing, "they created a way that it would drop partially down, perhaps a ledge or a sling of some type."

"I like the way you think. Let's start here. You go left, I'll go right."

On his hands and knees, Jeremy slowly began to move about the perimeter of the attic, setting aside junk as he worked. His headlamp only showed gloom descending into darkness between the wooden beams.

Fifteen minutes later, Steph called, "Jeremy! I found something!"

He joined her on the far side of the attic. Together they aimed their headlamps to the edge of the floor and beyond.

"Look, there are nails here holding thick strips of leather," Steph said, her voice pitched higher with excitement. "I'm afraid to pull on them for fear they'll break. They could be over a hundred years old!"

It looked like something, maybe a package, was hanging from the nails. "Perhaps if we each pull slowly and gently on the leather straps," he said, "it won't fall. And worse comes to worst, we can tear a hole in the wall below. It'll match all the others."

She took hold of the nearest strap, and he reached for the other one. Their heads touched, their shoulders touched. They were practically breathing in unison as they concentrated.

"Ready?" she said.

"Yep."

Slowly they lifted their straps.

"It doesn't feel as heavy as a book," she murmured.

"They're probably hand-written or typed pages."

When a wrapped package rose up over the edge of the attic floor, Steph reached for it. "Got it."

They sat back and looked at the burlap-wrapped package tied together with string.

"Don't breathe," he said, "or you might inhale a hundred years' worth of dust."

She smiled, then tipped the package sideways, trying to dislodge the worst of it. When she laid it down and began to gently pluck at the string, Jeremy pulled out a pocketknife and handed it to her.

With a quick slice, she was able to open the burlap wrapping to reveal a stack of papers an inch high. She turned it right side up and aimed her headlamp beam at it.

"Theodore Xu." She said the author's name with quiet reverence. "It's his lost work." She held it out to Jeremy silently.

To his surprise, he felt a tightness in his chest and swallowed heavily. The author had been a student of his great-great-grandmother. She had helped guide his talent, had agreed to protect his work while he risked his life fighting for a country that hadn't treated him or his ancestors like citizens.

"Wow," Jeremy breathed.

Steph smiled at him. "Kind of overwhelming."

"It is."

"Do you want to look at some of the pages? It doesn't seem too fragile."

He nodded and set the manuscript gently back onto its wrapping and turned over the first page. Side by side, they leaned over it, shoulders brushing, their twin headlamps illuminating this relic from the past. To his relief, the English words were typed rather than hand-written, and very legible. Perhaps the absence of light had kept it from fading. Silently, they read the first page, which began in the first person, with the author talking about his family in China. By the second page, it was obvious he was going to tell the story of his family's journey and their creation of a new home against daunting odds.

"Wow," Jeremy said again.

"Leaves you short on words." Steph chuckled.

He nudged her shoulder with his and she nudged back.

"He was a good writer, even as a teenager," Jeremy said. "This is an incredible find. I can't even imagine what the publishing world will make of this."

"Did he have descendants?"

"I don't know. But someone must be in charge of his estate." He gathered the pages back together, wrapped them in the burlap sack, then gave her a sympathetic look. "I hope the widows understand that this isn't the town's to sell."

Steph shrugged. "They know. But whose is it, really? Is it in the public domain? Finders keepers? What if there aren't any descendants?"

He smiled. "You're right. We really don't know."

"I'm sure the widows will find out. I think they were hoping that the lure of an incredible artifact at a future schoolhouse museum would be enough to gather more donors. I'll give them a call tonight so they can plan the next steps."

Together they gathered up all their supplies and loaded them into the car, taking special care of the manuscript. Steph held it in her lap as they drove the few minutes back to her apartment over the bakery. He pulled in the alley and up close to the door, then put it into park.

Jeremy looked over at her and realized she was staring back at him. For a long moment neither of them said anything as memories of their kiss rose up between them like smoke.

Did fate bring him back to her? The need to kiss her again was powerful, but he also knew that she didn't know how she felt as she emerged back into the dating world. Maybe she wasn't really ready, and their kiss had been more about gratitude that he'd saved her life.

While he was ruminating like an idiot, she leaned in, gave his cheek a quick kiss, and opened the car door.

"Thanks for all your help, Jeremy. I'll get back to you after I talk to the widows."

And then she was gone, and with a wince, he lowered his head to the steering wheel.

7

Monday morning, Jeremy was at his office computer between appointments, entering information about the last patient's MCL strain, when Janet Shaw leaned into his open doorway.

"Hey, Jeremy, Wendy Brissette just brought in little Avery Thalberg. She fell and bumped her head, and with both parents out of cellphone range, Wendy didn't want to take a chance. I assume you can see her right away? The next patient hasn't arrived yet."

"Of course, bring her into Exam Room 1."

He closed the patient's file on the computer, then walked down the old-fashioned hallway to the next exam room, which had probably been part of a parlor once, with bay windows curtained for privacy, polished wood floors, and a patterned tin ceiling.

Wendy sat in a chair next to the exam table, Avery straddling her lap, resting on her chest. Avery lifted her little head when Jeremy entered the room. Her eyes were wet and red, but her smile was big. A swollen bruise was already forming on her forehead.

"Hello, ladies," he said, pulling up the stool on wheels to sit down beside them.

Avery tucked her head back under Wendy's chin shyly. "Hi."

"I hear you fell," he continued.

Avery nodded solemnly. "It hurts."

"She tripped on a toy in the living room," Wendy said, her voice shaky. "I tried to keep an ice pack on it, but she wouldn't sit still long enough."

"Did she lose consciousness?"

Wendy shook her head.

Jeremy gave his patient a gentle smile. "Ice will make the bump feel better, Avery."

"But it's cold."

"Would you mind if I look in your eyes to make sure they weren't hurt in the fall?"

"Okay. But they don't hurt."

"I'm glad to hear it."

He shined a light in both her eyes, and they dilated normally. "Any vomiting or dizziness? Has she seemed alert and like her normal self?" he asked Wendy.

"She seems perfectly normal except for the bump. But...I didn't want to take a chance. I feel bad I worried her parents."

"Go ahead and leave another message that she's fine."

"Thanks." Wendy kissed Avery's forehead with obvious relief before lifting her phone to text one-handed.

The little girl looked between them before showing him her stuffed animal—a horse. He was always amazed at how much a toddler's wide, curious eyes could make him feel invited into a secret world.

"You really love horses," Jeremy said.

"Daddy said I can have my own when I'm big enough."

"Good for you."

Wendy cleared her throat, not quite meeting Jeremy's eyes. "Thank you for seeing us so quickly."

"Any time."

"Considering how I treated you last time we met..."

Jeremy smiled. "No need to worry about that."

"I'm sorry. It's just...it's been hard, you know?"

"I can say I understand your grief, but I truly can't know how you must feel, Wendy. I'm so sorry for all you've gone through. I wish...I wish things could have gone differently that day."

She nodded, then searched his eyes. "I hope you don't blame yourself."

"It's difficult not to," he murmured.

"Don't. It was an accident that no one could have predicted. You did what you could, and you saved Steph. That's important."

But I couldn't save your son, he thought, swallowing hard.

"Steph has been like my daughter since her teenage years."

"I know she doesn't want that to change. And it won't." And then he realized how that sounded. "I mean—not that I'm speaking for Steph, or even that—" He broke off when Wendy started chuckling.

"I totally understand. It's not like you need my permission to date her."

"*If* she'd date me—it's not like we've agreed to yet."

"But you're hoping?"

Jeremy felt his face get hot, and he prayed it wasn't too obvious. "Yes, I'm hoping."

"Good for you."

"Thank you, Wendy," he said quietly.

"I'd like us to be friends. I hope my behavior the other day won't make that impossible."

"Never."

He reached out his hand and, with a smile, she shook it.

Grinning, Avery put her hand on both of theirs, added her horse on top, and they all laughed.

~oOo~

Steph was surprised at how easy it was to give Jeremy a call that night as she lounged on her couch before the big window overlooking Main Street. She didn't second-guess herself, or wonder how it would be taken. The kiss they'd shared had seemed to change something inside her—how could it not, when it was all she'd thought about since Saturday?

When Jeremy answered, she could barely hear his voice over the loud music and conversations in the background.

"Hi, Steph!" he called, his voice raised.

"Hi, Jeremy. Sorry to call you at a bad time. Where are you?"

"The Wild Thing. My brother insisted I come. It's a lot of fun, even on a Monday night."

She thought of the crowded bar, the big dance floor, and the many women who'd be looking for a partner. The shot of jealousy took her by surprise.

"I can call you tomorrow," she began.

"No, that's okay. What can I do for you?"

"I wanted to thank you for how sweet you were with Avery today. Wendy spoke very highly of you. I think you have a fan. Or at least a nice review on your website."

"I'm glad to hear that Avery is so advanced."

She laughed, warmed by how light-hearted he could be. And then she said something she'd been debating, but hadn't decided on. "Do you have a group designing a sled to enter Sleddin' Like the Oldies?"

"I do. My brother and sister and me."

"That's great." Had she wanted him to be available? What was she thinking? "Well, you're welcome to attend our sled-building party at the Sweetheart Ranch. We're making an evening of it on Friday night."

"Why, Stephanie Brissette, are you inviting me on yet *another* date, before I've even had a chance to reciprocate?"

"You're just a little too slow, Doc."

His laughter, the warmth of flirty banter—she hadn't realized how much she'd missed it until Jeremy came back into her life.

"I was wracking my brain, trying to come up with ways I could put you to work on a date," he said, "the way you like to do to me."

"You think I'm putting you to work on our sled? I don't think my brothers will believe a doctor has the construction skills ranchers and builders do."

"Then I guess you'll have to come to the Chens' sled-building the following night and see what I'm capable of."

"I guess I'll have to. Have fun at The Wild Thing."

"You sure you don't want to join me?"

"I think two dates with you next weekend are about all my busy calendar can handle."

"You sound chicken to me. I do a mean country line dance."

"Really? Which one?"

He paused. "Don't force me to make you feel inferior."

"You can't even name one. Nice try, Doc. See you Friday at seven."

~oOo~

Steph drove up to the big two-story wooden barn at the Sweetheart Ranch. Jessica's car was already there, and she was looking at something on her phone when Steph gently tooted her horn.

Jessica's head came up, and she waved through the window.

Both of them slid on their gloves and got out of their warm cars. Their booted feet crunched against the packed snow.

"Brr," Jessica said, rubbing her upper arms through her coat.

"Let's get inside and get the heaters going."

Although the barn showed its age in the weathered wood on the outside, inside it had been totally renovated, with an open central floor and rows of empty horse stalls. Tall patio heaters were already positioned, thanks to her brothers.

Steph opened the propane tanks and lit the heating units rising above her head. "There we go. It'll be warm in no time. Let's bring out the goodies."

After setting up tables, they unloaded boxes from Sugar and Spice Sisters. Her brothers, Will, Chris, and Daniel, were bringing coolers of beer and soda. Steph and Jessica got the strings of lights stored in the office and began to hang them from the beams.

"It's so pretty you could have a wedding in here," Jessica said.

"So my catering sister-in-law Heather keeps telling my parents. But my dad and brothers are ranchers, not event coordinators. Or so says my brother Will."

Steph knew her family had begun to arrive when their white collie mixes, Boomer and Patton, came bounding through the door, followed by her parents. There were excited dogs wiggling against their legs as they tried to greet everyone, but eventually Steph gave up decorating and helped bring in even more food. Her brothers' wives and kids arrived, and Steph was busy refereeing at the dessert table and urging everyone to wait for the hamburgers and hotdogs her dad was grilling outside. The smell of cooking meat wafted in every time someone opened the door. Jessica darted here and there, taking photos for more fundraiser publicity.

Steph was about to reach for Will and Lindsey's six-month-old when voices became muted. One by one her brothers gave her raised eyebrows or murmured to each other, but she couldn't see what was going on.

And then like magic, her family members parted, and standing just inside the door was Jeremy, holding a platter of steaming hamburgers and hotdogs. When he saw her, his face lit up in a smile, and Steph heard Daniel snicker behind her.

"Daniel, I think Jeremy's here for you," Mom called.

"I didn't invite him," Daniel said, then added unhelpfully, "I wonder who did?"

Mom frowned, and then she saw where everyone was looking—and certainly she couldn't miss Steph's blush.

Steph moved through the crowd. "Hi, Jeremy."

He didn't try to give her a kiss, and she was mostly grateful. Mostly.

"Hi, Steph," he said. "I've been giving your dad a hand outside."

She took the platter from him and headed for the main food table. "Thanks for your help," she said over her shoulder. "Are you hungry?"

"After inhaling this for the last ten minutes, I think I am."

As she led him through the casual gauntlet of her family, Jeremy said hello several times. Her mom was beaming at her, eyes glistening. Steph steered Jeremy away from her for now.

At the food table, they lined up behind the kids and ended up each holding a plate for youngsters who couldn't scoop food and hold a plate at the same time. Jeremy waved away any parents who tried to help them, and she liked how he chatted with her nieces and nephews, surprisingly at ease. But then again, he had pint-sized patients.

When they had their own food, they sat on chairs, their plates on their laps, and talked to Daniel and his wife Kristin. Eventually Steph's parents joined them, and Steph steered the conversation to the sled they'd be building that night. Soon

Daniel was displaying his laptop where he'd designed their "winning entry."

"Wait," Jeremy began, "is that a boat? On skis?"

"It's an Old West theme, after all," Daniel said. "Can you guess what the boat represents?"

"Lewis and Clark!" yelled his oldest boy Justin. "We studied them in school this year. It was my idea. It was called a keel boat, and they built it in Pittsburgh."

"Wow," Jeremy said. "I'm impressed."

Soon they were dividing into teams, working on costumes or the snowboard base, or the boat itself. Steph and Jeremy worked on the base with Daniel, holding the frame together while Daniel drilled.

Eventually, when her brothers got together to attach the boat to the base, she grabbed Jeremy and pulled him outside.

The moon was nearly full in the black night sky, the stars so vivid they twinkled like Christmas lights as they walked away from the barn lights. Jeremy followed her without saying anything as she led him toward the corral where the horses, snug in their blankets, snuffled through the light snow looking for grass while they waited to be let back inside the barn. She rested her forearms on the fence and breathed deeply, enjoying the crisp cold air, with the view of the dark mountains blocking part of the sky.

"Sorry about my family," she finally said.

"Why should you be sorry? They've always been great."

"It was a little awkward when you arrived. They're just...well, I haven't dated anyone in a long time."

He bumped her elbow with his. "I know. Is it still awkward?"

She hesitated. "No," she whispered, turning to face him. The night shadows hid his eyes, showed his cheek bones in strong relief. She'd spent all evening watching him with her family, and it had felt so right. "You know, I had a crush on you when I was younger."

"I might have realized it."

She winced. "Was I that obvious?"

"I was flattered. I'm glad you're all grown up now."

This time, she was the one who leaned in for a kiss. His mouth was so warm, his nose and chin cold. When he slid his arms around her, she molded against him like they belonged pressed together. They spent long moments learning each other's kisses, tongues meeting, moans exchanged.

It was Jeremy who lifted his head at last. "I could do this forever, but perhaps you wouldn't want the teasing when we've been gone too long from the party."

She laughed shakily. "Let them think what they like. I'm an adult."

"But to our parents, we're forever their children."

"And they worry." She sighed and snuggled her head beneath his chin, enjoying the feel of his strength all around her. "Then let's talk about something other than us. I spoke with the widows about the manuscript. They talked to Kate De Luca, our local lawyer—you remember her, right? She contacted Theodore Xu's publishing house."

"That's a trail of connections," he said.

His voice rumbled in his chest pleasurably beneath her ear.

"The publisher is now contacting the author's estate, and we'll see what happens from there. Until then, the manuscript is in a safety deposit box at the bank."

"It looks like everything has been put in motion," he said. "I'm sure the estate won't mind sharing the manuscript for the occasional exhibit."

"The widows are hoping to get permission to mention the manuscript at the fundraiser. Our names might be brought up as the people who found it."

"Do you mind?"

She lifted her head and looked up at him. "No. Do you?"

His grin was slow, his shadowed gaze focused on her mouth. "Hell, no. The only thing I'll mind is if you don't let me kiss you again."

A sudden nudge to their shoulders seemed to startle Jeremy, but Steph knew immediately what it was. Her horse had come over to say hello.

She rubbed the bridge of the mare's nose. "Hello, Raia, you good girl." She glanced at Jeremy, who put his hand almost experimentally on Raia's neck.

"Is Raia the horse you competed with at barrel racing?"

She nodded. "She's as competitive as I am."

"I thought Daniel told me you continued competing after high school."

"I did, but it was difficult during college. I attended some events in the summer, but I was also working at Sugar and Spice. My focus wasn't there. After graduation, we got married, and there was the bakery and..." Her voice trailed off.

"Do you miss it?" he asked quietly.

"I do. I think I'm ready to give it more time." She gave him a teasing smile. "You told me you've never ridden. Maybe we should give it a try."

"Maybe not at night."

She chuckled. "Well, that makes sense, I suppose. What about you and skiing? I imagine there was so much extra time in medical school."

He laughed. "So much time. And that's a lie."

"No. I'm shocked."

"That's one of the things I plan to rectify, now that I don't have to study as much. Maybe you'd join me?"

Her smile faded. "I haven't skied since Tyler died." When the words came out of her mouth, she was stunned. "I'm sorry, Jeremy. I really know how to ruin the mood."

He took her cold hand between his. "Don't apologize. We've spent the evening talking about a race that's going to take place on a ski slope. It's only natural it would occur to you."

"I wasn't even thinking much about it before tonight." She glanced at the barn, where light streamed from every crack around windows and doors, as if it glowed. She could hear her family inside, the murmur of their voices raised in excitement and laughter. "I was all in, planning what I'll wear, how I'll help steer."

"Maybe that's a good sign, that you're ready to. Or you could always be too busy coordinating the day with the widows if you want to stay off the hill."

"No. It's time. Tyler wouldn't have wanted me to stop doing" —she cleared her throat—"something we both loved to do."

Jeremy squeezed her hand a little tighter, and his presence was so comforting, she barely held back the words, *It's all my fault. He's dead because of me.*

But she'd never said them out loud, not to her family, not to her best friends. And here she'd thought about telling Jeremy. What would he think of her?

Was that part of why she held back? How had he become so important in her life in only a few weeks?

"Let's go back inside," she said, letting go of his hand.

The rest of the evening was devoted to painting and decorating their sled, while Mom took turns fitting everyone in the costumes she'd found online. When things were winding down, Steph walked Jeremy to the door but didn't go outside to say good-bye. On impulse, she gave him a quick kiss, and he smiled as he zipped up his coat and headed out into the cold.

She took a deep breath, bracing herself, before turning and facing her family again. She was surprised when none of them made any comment that she was dating—they were just putting away tools and cleaning up the rare paint splotch on the cement floor. She told herself she was relieved and joined in to help.

But *was* she relieved? Had she *wanted* them to tease her, to act like she was normal again—whatever that meant.

"Steph, can you help me carry the food trays back to the house?" Mom asked.

Steph dutifully gathered the empty platters and leftover paper plates and napkins. She followed her mom up the path to the big house, small light posts guiding the way.

Once in the kitchen, Steph filled the sink to start washing platters, feeling her mother's gaze on her. Steph focused on the crystal hanging in the darkened window in front of her. Every window in the house sparkled during the day with a crystal. Her mom was a partner in the Mystic Connection, a New Age shop that fit her bohemian lifestyle. She treated her family almost like a commune, where everyone knew everyone's business.

"So...Jeremy..." Mom began.

Steph smiled at her over her shoulder. "Yep. Jeremy."

"You're dating?"

Steph tried not to smile at the hopeful sound of her mother's voice. "Kind of. It's new."

"I'm glad. How does it feel?"

"Strange." Steph plunged her hands into the soapy water, looking for the sponge. "But I had to try again sometime."

Mom leaned her hip against the counter near Steph, the flowing sleeves of her dress just missing the sink. "I admit when you were so active with the fundraiser with the widows, I wondered if you related to them a little too much."

"Because I'm a widow?"

Mom nodded, then accepted a dripping platter and began to dry it off. "I worried that you didn't want to date again."

"The widows have actually been pushing me to date."

Mom smiled. "Well, then, I was wrong."

"Not quite." Steph soaped another platter. "I've been giving that a lot of thought—maybe I felt a little too safe with them, with being like them."

"No one would blame you for that," her mother said softly. "You needed time."

"I did. Dealing with all this has been hard. I don't know if I'll ever truly get over the senselessness of Tyler's death."

"I don't think we ever forget trauma and grief," her mom said slowly, her gaze distant. "But I think time fuzzies the edges of those memories, makes them not hurt quite so much. It doesn't mean we forget the love we lost, but we find a way to be grateful we had it."

Grateful. Steph didn't know how to get past her guilt to feel grateful. She hadn't even been able to explain it all to the therapist she'd seen the first year after Tyler's death. She opened her mouth, willing the words to unburden themselves to her mother, but...she couldn't. Guilt, cowardice, fear—they were all mixed up inside her mind. She hoped that taking the next step with Jeremy would help her move on, but deep inside, she feared it would never happen.

But she couldn't burden her mom like that.

"Thanks for the advice, Mom," she murmured, then forced a smile. "'Fuzzies the edges'? That's a phrase, all right."

Mom laughed. "I have a way with words."

Steph gave her mom a hug. "Love you."

8

Jeremy was surprised at how nervous he was, waiting for Steph to arrive at his parents'. It felt so much more important than a random date. He kept busy, helping his mom bring the Lumpia spring rolls to their two-car garage, where they'd decided to build the sled. He fiddled with space heaters, trying to get the temperature above sixty degrees.

"It's a little pathetic to see our older brother in such a state," Eric said.

Startled, Jeremy turned around to see his brother and sister standing just inside the door, looking at him with sly amusement.

"I'm not in any kind of state," Jeremy said mildly.

Eric rubbed his chin thoughtfully. "Isn't Steph Brissette joining us?"

"She is."

Eric and Brianna exchanged another knowing look.

"I think it's cute," Brianna said. She wore a winter headband covering her ears, and her dark ponytail bounced at the back of her head. "It's like you're human after all. I think this is the first time you've brought home a woman."

Jeremy rolled his eyes. "When have I not been human?"

"Maybe when you graduated first in your college class?" Eric said.

"Or first in your medical school class," Brianna chimed in.

"I didn't brag about that," Jeremy insisted.

"No, Mom did." Eric shook his head.

"And that was worse." Brianna sighed. The she brightened. "But now you're in a state over a woman, and I'm feeling good about life again."

Jeremy sighed. "Why don't you help me finish getting the food ready."

"I think the sled is more important," Eric said, looking down at the collection of lumber.

"But this is a date." Brianna linked her arm with Jeremy's. "Food is more important. A happy date leads to..." She trailed off. "Never mind. Gross."

Jeremy couldn't resist a laugh.

When everything was ready, his parents continued to fuss over the food as his siblings laid out their building plans. Maybe their sled-building wasn't taking place in a big modern barn that looked like a Pinterest wedding photo shoot, but they knew how to get things done.

Brianna nudged him in the ribs. "Look who's at the door!"

Jeremy turned around fast, only to hear Brianna's soft laughter as he went to greet Steph. She was wearing jeans and a light zipped sweatshirt over a flannel buttoned down shirt, ready to do physical work, and he thought she couldn't have looked more beautiful.

Once Steph had greeted his family, she stood over the lumber piled against the wall beneath mounted gardening tools. "So what are you building?"

"I hope you don't have any plans to sabotage the competition," Jeremy said.

She laughed. "No need. The Sweets are in it to win it."

"We'll see. I think we have a better shot at the style points. Our cart has a local theme."

"Oh, interesting strategy. So what's local?"

"Here's a hint." Brianna laid out two lengths of wood, then began to crisscross it with more. "Do you have a guess?"

"Railroad tracks," Steph said. "So this will be a train?"

They all shook their heads.

"What else uses..." Steph expression lightened. "Mining carts use train tracks. Oh, good call."

They began to build, and although Steph laughed along with the rest every time they made a mistake, Jeremy felt a distance between them that hadn't been there at the Sweetheart Ranch the previous night. It had only been twenty-four hours—what could have possibly changed?

When the mining cart had been constructed, and Brianna and Eric were choosing the paint colors they intended to buy the next day, Jeremy helped dispose of the trash. Steph followed him outside, her hands in her pockets, her breath misting as he tossed a trash bag in the bin and firmly locked it to keep bears away.

They looked up at the dark sky with its explosion of starlight, something so vivid in Valentine Valley, but muted in Denver. He never got over the wonder of it. He heard Steph sigh, and suddenly he wanted to distract her.

"I have a key to my new house," he said.

She gave him an interested smile. "You signed the papers already?"

"No, but the owners moved out, and they're friends of my parents, so...you want to see it?"

"Sounds like the widows aren't the only ones with suspiciously procured keys." Her smile broadened. "But I'm in."

They retrieved their coats and assured the family they'd be back.

Outside he said, "The house is on the far side of Main Street, near the Rose Garden. I could drive, since it's so cold."

"Let's walk. I love the stillness of a winter evening."

"That's practically poetic."

She shrugged, laughing softly, and they began to walk. It was only five blocks away, and Jeremy didn't have the heart to break the silence she enjoyed. On a Saturday evening, Main Street was bustling as people walked between restaurants, bars, and stores, with tiny white lights in the trees a reminder that Christmas had only just passed. As they entered a residential neighborhood, the quiet returned.

A block later, he pointed out the small two-story home.

"Oh, it fronts the park itself," Steph said. "How wonderful."

He led the way up the front stairs onto the porch, where a light illuminated his search for the right key. The lock turned silently, and he pushed the door open. Steph followed him in and stood beside him on the mat that protected the wood floors. Moonlight shone through the windows in beams that cut through the shadows. There was an echoing emptiness to the house, as if it was hushed and waiting for new life.

Jeremy and Steph took off their boots and coats and left them by the door, traipsing from room to room in their socks. She complimented the new tile in the bathrooms and the layout of the kitchen.

When they returned to the living room, she stood at the large front window. "Turn off the light so we can see the garden."

He did as she asked, watching shadows settle around her as he moved to her side. Now they could see the old-fashioned lamps that marked the boundary of the Rose Garden and lined several pathways through the landscape, as well as marking each end of the small bridge.

"You will love this view," she said quietly, her breath like a gentle sigh.

Their arms brushed as they stood side by side. They were alone, the house hushed, the snow beginning to fall outside as if adding more white to the canvas that was Valentine Valley.

Jeremy took her hand. She squeezed his, then turned to face him. Her lovely face was ethereal in the shadows, half dark, the other half in moonlit glow. He leaned down and kissed her softly. When her hands settled on his waist, he cupped her face and deepened the kiss. He lost awareness of himself and the world as he explored her. He slid his hands to her shoulders and then down her back, pulling their bodies together. The touch of her warm curves made him groan, but he forced himself to take his time, when all he wanted to do was find the nearest bed.

That thought brought him back to their surroundings. He lifted his head and managed a wry smile, even as his breathing was labored. "Once again, we're kissing in a place not exactly conducive to romance."

"I don't care," she whispered as she slid her hand behind his neck and pulled him back down for another kiss.

When she moaned into his mouth, he lost the ability to think. All he could do was explore, needing to touch every part of her. His hands roamed her hips and backside, even as she caressed his face, his neck, his chest. Their mouths slanted across each other's, their ragged breathing merged, and he let his hands slide up her ribcage to cup her breasts.

She gasped and leaned into him. "Yes."

Through her clothes, he felt the hard point of her nipples against his palms. He tweaked them as he spread kisses across her cheek and down her neck. He needed to be closer, to touch every part of her. He unzipped her sweatshirt slowly, giving her a chance to object, but she didn't. Her eyes were closed, her expression intent and yearning.

Kneeling down, he unbuttoned her flannel shirt and buried his face between her lace-covered breasts. She arched, head leaning back, and he took one nipple into his mouth through her delicate bra. When she cried out and shuddered, he reached up and played with her other breast. He slid his tongue beneath the edge. It wouldn't take much to slide the cup aside and—

Steph suddenly stumbled back, pulling her shirt together.

Caught by surprise, still kneeling, Jeremy stared at her. "Is something wrong?"

She shook her head, buttoning her shirt with fingers that obviously trembled. "Nothing wrong, nothing at all. It's just...me."

"This isn't the most romantic place—"

"Please don't make excuses for me," she whispered harshly. She found her coat on the floor behind her, slid into it, then tried to step into her boots. But they refused to cooperate, and she struggled to loosen the laces.

By this time, he was on his feet and approaching her as if she was a volcano that might go off. "There's no need to rush out of here. Let's talk."

"I—I can't." She got her last boot on and finally met his eyes in the shadowy gloom. "I don't know if I'm ready—if I'll *ever* be ready. You deserve better than someone who—"

"Don't say it. I want you, Stephanie Brissette, and that means I want everything you are, everything you feel. I'm not here for a one-night stand. Hell, I've brought you to my parents—twice. That should tell you my commitment. And I'm willing to do anything or wait as long as necessary to make you feel comfortable. We're not on the clock here."

She bit her lip and tried to smile, but he could see tears sparkling in her lashes.

"Thanks. Can we talk later?"

She opened the front door and darted out so fast he was caught unaware. He didn't even have his boots on.

"Steph, wait! Let me walk you back to your car!"

She spun in a circle even as she headed through the snow covering the front walkway. "I didn't drive my car. I walked. I'll talk to you later."

And while he hopped one-footed trying to put on his boots, she put her hands into her pockets, her coat flapping, and practically ran. He gave up and leaned against the doorjamb, watching her, shaking his head.

But he wasn't discouraged, and he wasn't going to give up.

As Steph decorated cookies to be sold at the fundraiser the next day, the feelings of guilt and frustration that had been dogging her all week continued to hover like a dark cloud over her head. She'd texted back and forth with Jeremy regularly, but dodged even a coffee date, claiming she was too busy prepping for the big event.

It wasn't a lie, but...an exaggeration. And all because she couldn't face how much she'd almost dragged Jeremy down to the floor to make love—and then how she'd pulled back with little explanation. Her need for him had taken her by surprise, but surely there had been a better way to handle her worry that it was too much, too fast.

And now the longer she put off discussing it with him in person, the more awkward and unsure she felt.

Why would he want to date someone as hot and cold as she was?

No, the real truth was why would he want to date someone who was lying to him? Okay, maybe that was harsh, but she was definitely withholding a vital truth that had formed the foundation of her grief this last year and a half.

Her feelings of guilt in her husband's death.

She couldn't go on like this. She had to say the words out loud, to let Jeremy know the kind of person she was so that he could make an honest decision about dating her.

And she wanted him to decide that she was still worth it.

There, that was the crux of the issue. Would he decide her mistakes were forgivable? Had she concluded that for herself?

Before she could overthink and talk herself out of it, she glanced at the clock on the kitchen wall. It was after six and she hadn't even noticed the dinner hour come and go. Emily had said good-bye in a rush, something about Nate and Avery waiting, and Steph had barely heard her.

Steph had to get out of this mindset where she was just hovering above her life like an onlooker, not truly living it.

She called Jeremy, and he answered immediately.

"Hi, Steph."

His voice was warm and welcoming and sexy. He made her blush, and she found it endearing.

"Hi, Jeremy. I was wondering what your plans are for the big day tomorrow?"

"Except for competing in the race, I'm pretty open. I was hoping I could spend some of the day with you."

"I'd like that, too." He was so easy to talk to, so understanding. He hadn't pushed her this week about why she'd run out on him after his great kisses and...everything else. It had been difficult to sleep that night, her body so alive and aware of what it had been missing—of what Jeremy could make her feel.

"Let me help at your booth tomorrow," he said. "I passed by the bottom of the slope in Aspen earlier today, and an entire village of booths has sprung up."

"We could use the help selling cookies, thanks."

"Want to ride up valley together?"

She hesitated. That was twenty minutes of alone time. What

was she so afraid of? "That would be great. I'll drive. I'll have a lot of cookie boxes already in the car. It makes a great refrigerator. Can you be at the bakery at 8?"

"I'll be there."

"Good night, Jeremy, and thanks." She heard her voice get all soft and mushy. My God, she was falling hard and fast.

"Good night, Steph."

~oOo~

It was a hectic morning in Aspen. Since it was the height of ski season, tourists strolled along the Cooper Avenue pedestrian mall in their ski pants and jackets. Steph really enjoyed the looks they gave the Sleddin' Like the Oldies participants when they walked by. There were saloon girls with petticoats ruffling their skirts over their ski pants, Union soldiers with their blue caps and epaulettes on their uniform coats. Jeremy and his siblings wore trousers, suspenders, and rough jackets over their long johns, with headlamps on their ski helmets. Steph loved the fringed buckskin jackets and pants that she and her brothers wore.

As she and Jeremy made their way toward the fundraising booths, the tourists asked about their costumes, then happily followed to patronize the booths, buy tickets for the competition, and raise money for the schoolhouse.

They walked past woodcrafters, jewelry artists, and cheese makers to find a smiling Emily manning the cookie booth. She was wearing a prairie dress and bonnet, but all across her costume small paper squares had been glued, the colors matching whatever they were affixed to. Even her bonnet had little squares. Steph laughed when she saw Jeremy's puzzled expression.

He gave Emily a once-over. "And what are you supposed to be?"

"You can't guess?" Emily said, even as she thanked a customer and returned their credit card.

"I think he lacks imagination." Steph conspiratorially elbowed her sister. "It's all that scientific training."

"Okay, I lack imagination," Jeremy said, smiling. "What are you and your friends supposed to be?"

"Early settlers, of course," Emily said. "We followed the Oregon Trail."

He blinked and looked her up and down once more. "You don't mean...the old video game, The Oregon Trail?"

"I'm pixilated!" Emily said with a giggle.

"I tried to tell her that a video game doesn't count as an Old West theme," Steph teased.

"Does too! Dysentery and cholera were very Old West," her sister responded. Then she looked past Steph to the patient Aspen tourists lined up behind her. "If you two are helping, let's get to it. We have a lot of cookies to sell before the main event this afternoon."

Steph spent a pleasant but busy hour side by side with Emily and Jeremy. She and Jeremy didn't even have to be focusing on each other for her to enjoy his company. He'd made her laugh on their car ride to Aspen, telling stories about unusual ER patients including one who repeatedly ran around naked. Emily kept sneaking looks at him, then giving Steph wide-eyed, excited gazes behind his back. Steph only rolled her eyes in return, but she was smiling. It was so good to feel happy and intrigued.

Their next customer was an Asian-American man in his fifties wearing a buttoned-up trench coat with a scarf wrapped several times around his neck.

"Are you Stephanie Brissette?" he asked Emily.

"That's my sister," Emily said, gesturing with her thumb at Steph.

"Can I help you?" Steph asked.

"I'm Vincent Xu."

Steph exchanged a look with Jeremy. "Your last name is Xu?"

"Theodore Xu was my grandfather," Mr. Xu said. "I understand you're the lady who found his first manuscript?"

Steph's smile slowly widened. "I did—we did," she added quickly, elbowing Jeremy. "I didn't know he had descendants."

"I'm the only one left. I read the entire manuscript after I arrived yesterday. Were you able to read it?"

She shook her head.

"It tells how our family first came to this country, expanding on things my grandfather had said. But I was a little boy when he died, and he was a private man, and well—" His voice choked up, and he added huskily, "I feel like I've gotten a part of my family back, and you've both given that to me."

Steph's eyes grew watery, and she wanted to hug him.

Mrs. Palmer came up behind him, a frilly flower-covered hat perched on top of her big blond wig. "I've been escortin' Mr. Xu around, but he most specifically wanted to meet the two of you. Why don't you go talk, and I'll help Emily?"

They led Mr. Xu to a nearby picnic table, then answered his questions about how they found the manuscript, and how they even knew one existed when he didn't. He was fascinated by Jeremy's family history, which tied into the memoir his grandfather had written.

"I'm sorry you didn't get a chance to read it," Mr. Xu said.

Jeremy shrugged. "We thought it best to keep it protected until we contacted his heirs."

"I will make a copy for you," Mr. Xu said. "I'm so amazed and grateful you reached out to me, when you could have done what you wanted with the manuscript."

"We thought it was only right. And we can wait for the book," Steph insisted. "There will be a book, right?"

He laughed. "Oh, there'll be a book. I'm making a copy today to send to an agent. My grandfather's publisher recommended several that I could interview, and I'll do my own research. I want someone who can represent the book and do it justice, rather than focus on how much money it can make." He leaned toward them. "And it's going to make a lot of money. I don't need much myself, so I'm excited to research charities that have meaning to Asian Americans—and also to our history." He glanced at Jeremy. "Which means that the Valentine Valley school house where my grandfather learned to write from your great-great-grandmother will definitely be moved and taken care of. I'm honored to be a part of such a community effort."

Steph's throat constricted as she watched the two men of different generations regard each other with sober understanding and respect. They shared a bond they hadn't known about. Jeremy and his family would always know that they played a part in revealing another immigrant story that helped shape America.

Jeremy glanced at her and smiled gently. "Need a tissue?"

She hadn't even realized her tears had spilled over. She laughed and accepted, and Mr. Xu looked on with a compassionate, understanding gaze.

~oOo~

As the morning wore on, and the crowds grew and swarmed the base of the sled course, Steph finally began to look at what she'd avoided—the mountain, a conquering god rising up above her. The ski trails flowed like serpentine snow rivers, smaller streams cutting through the fir trees lining the main runs. Above and beyond lay even more of the mountain that you couldn't see from below. It felt like a hidden monster, waiting for her to get too close. Her mouth was so dry she couldn't swallow.

She took a deep breath and closed her eyes, reminding herself that she'd spent every winter of her entire life skiing these resorts. They'd given her the joy of gorgeous views from the summit and brisk, windy runs down the mountainside feeling the thrill of competition as she raced her brothers.

But a mountain like this had taken her husband's life cruelly and without warning. For months as she struggled to accept his death, she'd prayed that he'd been unconscious, that he hadn't felt the panic of smothering. Her nightmares had been full of the opposite.

She hadn't wanted to ski again—it had been easy at first to avoid it. Everyone understood. But when the newest season began a few months ago, she'd felt everyone's pity and worry when they asked her to ski and she declined, always with a ready reason. After Christmas, they'd just stopped asking. And maybe that was worse. She sensed they were hiding their ski trips from her and feeling guilty. She didn't want to be a burden, to know that her family couldn't enjoy their own days on the slopes as much because she was hiding from them.

She'd decided weeks ago that this fundraiser would begin her turnaround. She'd told her brothers she'd be riding the sled, too. She wasn't certain they believed her; maybe they were humoring her, assuming she'd back out. She wasn't going to do that. Now the sleds were waiting at the top of one of the lower slopes, pulled up there by snowcats. She was waiting in line to jump on another snowcat for the ride up the hill, feeling resolute, though her insides trembled.

"How are you doing?" Jeremy asked quietly.

He was at her side as he had been all morning, a supportive, calm presence. Ahead of them her family members were scattered up and down the line, as were his. Emily looked over her shoulder and gave her a cheerful smile that was still tinged with a worry she couldn't hide.

"I'm okay," Steph said to Jeremy. "Although it's not a pleasant feeling being my family's focus today. And you don't have to say it—I know they're worried and that they love me."

Beneath that silly headlamp on his helmet, Jeremy was looking at her so gently that she held her breath, as if he might admit to loving her, too. But he didn't, to her relief. And she *was* relieved, she insisted silently. Or was she?

"It'll be good to show them you've taken a solid step forward," he continued. "And you won't be skiing at all, just going down on a sled."

"Uh huh," she said agreeably.

But it wasn't really the skiing itself. It was the mountain, wild and unpredictable and capable of falling away underneath your feet, roaring down behind you like the Four Horsemen of the Apocalypse. Her heart pounded in her chest.

"You look a little pale," Jeremy said.

She took a deep breath and forced a smile. "I'm fine, Doc. What's taking so long up there?"

J eremy knew he was beginning to get on Steph's nerves with his concern. She was working hard at feeling normal, like everyone else enjoying a fun day on the slopes, and he admired her for her bravery. If a mountain of snow fell on him, almost crushed and smothered him, then took the life of someone he loved, he didn't know how he would manage to recover. But she had. And she would get through this day and be all the better for it. He had confidence in her.

She was silent as they perched on the trailer behind the snowcat, her expression almost blank as the Roaring Fork Valley dropped away behind them. The wind picked up and turned colder.

"It's the breath of the mountain," she murmured.

Jeremy felt like he read her lips more than heard her over the engines. "Maybe you should take up writing. That's pretty descriptive."

She met his gaze from behind her goggles and gave a faint smile. "When a mountain has a starring role in your nightmares for months, it takes on mythic qualities."

"Do you still have the nightmares?"

"Not so much, and not last night, which was surprising. But maybe my nightmares know I've moved past them."

"That's good."

"Yes, Doctor."

He chuckled, and tension eased in his chest. He wanted her to feel happy and whole and glad to be alive. If he didn't get to be a part of her world, he would find a way to be okay with that, as long as he knew she'd recovered.

God, he sounded lovesick, even to himself.

The snowcat took them beyond the starting line, where all the sleds waited, a riotous mix of color and shapes, made of everything from metal to cardboard. There was even a Trojan horse, and Josh Thalberg was telling everyone who'd listen that no one had specified which West, nor what year.

Soon they were separated into groups, positioning their sleds in order of descent, talking and laughing. Jeremy watched as Steph was enveloped into the warmth of her family. Her oldest brother Will had somehow managed to affix a coonskin cap to his ski helmet, and Steph laughed so hard she had to bend over and brace herself on her knees.

Jeremy relaxed and got to work with his own family, trying to duct tape one of the railroad ties, which had come loose from the old ski they were using as a runner.

His team was one of the first down the slope to be judged, and it was a wild ride, as his sister Brianna and brother Eric rode inside the mining cart, and he held onto the rear, using the "brakes" they added to each side of the cart to dig into the snow. The lower part of the slope was crowded with people who'd hiked up to get a closer look at the action, and down below, he could see hundreds of people waving their arms. Their cheers rose up to echo through the valley.

Near the bottom, the slope flattened out and Jeremy had to abandon the jury-rigged brakes to drag his foot and slow the sled down the old-fashioned way. Eric jumped out of the cart to do the same thing and almost took a tumble, laughing as he braced himself next to Jeremy. They managed to avoid the line of safety fencing.

As they came to a stop, the announcers were describing their mining cart sled and expressing amazement at their speed. The Chens pumped their fists and played to the crowd, even as they pushed their sled off to the side for the next group.

Emily's team came down next, their cardboard Conestoga wagon mounted on two snowboards and affixed with hundreds of pixilated squares. Jeremy didn't even have to explain the video game theme to Eric and Brianna, who got it right away.

When the announcers called the Sweetheart Ranch entry, Jeremy pushed through the crowd so he could be at the front. He saw that a special chair had been placed in the front row nearby for Mrs. Sweet, the matriarch of the ranch family. She'd dressed herself in the finest Victorian fashions, including a wide-brimmed hat dripping with artificial flowers, and layers of flowing silk skirts, unlike her friendly rivals, the Widows, who still sported the prairie wardrobe theme they'd been wearing everywhere for a month. They had determination, those women. The widows were in the judges' booth, giving their opinion on everything, and more than once, Mrs. Palmer, the spokesperson of the group, took over the microphone.

Jeremy watched the Lewis and Clark homage, a boat on a snowboard, come down the hill, three Sweets in the boat, and one at the back end to slow things down as needed. One of the oars had been affixed to the lead runner, and though they tried to make it look like Steph's brother Chris was rowing, he was really trying to steer. They raced a wild zigzag down the slope, and just as they'd almost come to a complete stop, Chris steered too hard and the boat "capsized."

Jeremy rushed forwarded with several others to right the

ship, and the Sweets tumbled clear, laughing. Steph ended up in a pile of snow, and as Jeremy reached her, she was trying to clear it from her face frantically. He dropped to his knees beside her, pulled off his gloves, and gently wiped the last snow from her face.

He cupped her cold cheeks with his warm hands and looked through her goggles into her eyes. "Hey, I got you. Good job."

She blinked and nodded. After she took off her gloves, she lifted her goggles onto her helmet. Color was coming back into her face in red splotches, and her heavy breathing was subsiding.

"You okay?" he asked.

"Yeah, I guess I am." She started unbuckling her helmet.

"Should we go get some hot chocolate?" he asked.

She nodded again but didn't speak. Her brothers had gathered around her with concern, her parents and grandma stiffly waiting at the edge of the crowd. Then Steph smiled and waved, and a visible ripple of relief spread out around her. She handed her helmet to Daniel.

"We'll be back soon," Jeremy called, and took her by the hand.

They lined up for hot chocolate at one of the booths, then he led her toward the picnic tables. They sat on the same side of the table, and for a few minutes, they blew on their hot chocolate and then risked a sip. She watched the next race, her lips lifted in the occasional brief smile, but her brow was furrowed.

"Did you enjoy the ride down the course?" he finally asked.

She glanced at him for a long moment, then set down her cup. "I did. When we tipped over, I wasn't really scared—we were going so slow—but then when my face hit the snow...I flashed back to that day."

He nodded. "But you worked your way through it."

"Really?" she asked wryly. "It didn't feel that way. It's been hovering over me for a year and a half. The guilt has been almost more than I can bear, although rest assured, I do feel better."

"Survivor's guilt is only natural," he began.

She held up a hand. "It's not survivor's guilt—well, okay, there's some of that, too. It's worse than that—the whole vacation was my idea."

He inwardly winced but remained quiet.

"I've never told anyone about this," she said, her voice low and threaded with pain. "It's been hard to admit to myself. The vacation was my attempt to bring romance back into our lives. We—we'd only ever dated each other, and I was starting to worry that we'd gotten married too soon, that maybe I didn't love Tyler as deeply as I thought." Her voice broke and when she squeezed her eyes shut, a tear leaked out.

Jeremy reached for her hand in both of his and squeezed gently. He ached down to his soul for the pain she'd gone through, the grief that had twisted into guilt.

"He didn't even want to go," she whispered, bowing her head. "He did it for me, because he would always do anything to make me happy." A sob escaped and she covered her mouth.

"Steph, sweetheart, forgive me for saying what you've probably heard from so many others, but he wanted you to be happy. You wanted to strengthen and improve your marriage. You could have been a person who ran away, who took the easy way out and distanced yourself, asked for a trial separation, but instead you tried to make things better, because you loved him."

She covered her face with both hands, and he put his arm around her trembling shoulders.

"I did love him," she whispered. "I was so sad to think I might not have loved him enough."

"That's not true. I saw you both that morning in the lodge."

She turned to face him, lips parted, eyes red. "I don't remember seeing you."

He gave her a smile. "That's because you were so wrapped up in each other. You looked so in love and happy."

She bit her lip, and more tears spilled. "I wanted to be. I would have done anything to make our life together even happier." She took a deep, shaky breath. "Thank you for listening."

"Any time." He slid his arms from around her shoulders, but kept their hands joined.

For several minutes, they drank their hot chocolate and watched the last sleds compete. Jeremy thought her gaze was a little unfocused, but he hoped she was reexamining all the thoughts she'd tortured herself with and beginning the journey to let them fade away. She deserved a long, full, happy life— Tyler would have wanted that for her. Jeremy did, too.

~oOo~

At the end of the afternoon, Steph stood beside Jeremy, feeling calm and at peace for the first time in a long while. The widows announced the various winners for the day: Most Creative, Fastest, Sturdiest, Best Dressed. Emily and her best friends won Most Creative for their Oregon Trail video game theme. Jeremy's mouth dropped open when his family's mining cart had the fastest time.

Steph elbowed him and couldn't resist saying, "Winning isn't as important as all the money that was raised to preserve Valentine Valley's history."

Jeremy's expression sobered as he nodded, but she loved the twinkle in his eye.

Steph was glad to have helped in more ways than one. Without the manuscript and Mr. Xu's generosity, they might have been able to move the building, but preserving and reopening it could have taken decades.

She slid her arm around Jeremy's waist, tucking herself beneath his shoulder. He looked down at her and smiled with such tenderness that it took her breath away. Relief continued to flow through her, rejuvenating her. He'd listened to all of her heartache and had said just the right things. He didn't think her a terrible person who couldn't be redeemed.

"And lastly," Mrs. Thalberg said, her bonnet falling back from her red hair, "I want to remind you all that in saving our past, we learn to understand where we came from. It doesn't mean we live in the past—"

Steph held her breath, because it seemed like the widow was looking straight at her.

"—but we can understand and accept what it was to us, flaws and all, while still moving into the future."

Everyone clapped and cheered, and once again, Steph felt her eyes blurring with tears. What did her mom always say—something about being a watering pot? That was Steph today.

Jeremy squeezed her against his side. She looked up into his smiling face, and on impulse, she came up on her tiptoes and pulled his head down for a kiss. She'd taken him by surprise, but he joined in eagerly, his mouth warm against hers on the cold winter day.

When they broke the kiss, she kept her hand on his cheek and looked into his eyes. "You're pretty amazing," she said.

"You, too."

"A woman could fall in love with a man like you."

"Could she?" There was a note of sincerity in his voice in the midst of their teasing.

"She could."

"A man could soon be hopelessly in love with a woman like you, too," he said quietly.

"I think that's a good start."
They both leaned in for another kiss.

THE END

THANK you for taking the time to read **A SECOND CHANCE IN VALENTINE VALLEY.** If you enjoyed it, please consider telling your friends or posting a short review where you bought it. Word of mouth is an author's best friend and much appreciated.

Thank you!
Emma Cane

BOOKS BY EMMA CANE

The Fairfield Orchard series

At Fairfield Orchard

A Spiced Apple Winter

The Apple Blossom Café

The Valentine Valley series

A Town Called Valentine

True Love at Silver Creek Ranch

The Cowboy of Valentine Valley

A Promise at Bluebell Hill

Sleigh Bells in Valentine Valley

Ever After at Sweetheart Ranch

Novellas in the Valentine Valley series

"The Christmas Cabin"

(from the *All I Want For Christmas Is a Cowboy* anthology)

A Wedding in Valentine

When the Rancher Came to Town

Secrets in Valentine Valley

ABOUT THE AUTHOR

Emma Cane grew up reading and soon discovered that she liked to write passionate stories of teenagers in space. Her love of "passionate stories" has never gone away, although today she concentrates on the heartwarming characters of Valentine Valley and Fairfield Orchard.

Now that her three children are grown, Emma loves spending time crocheting and singing (although not necessarily at the same time), and hiking and snowshoeing alongside her husband Jim and their rambunctious dog, Uma.

Emma also writes *USA Today* bestselling historical romances under the name Gayle Callen.

Visit Emma's website: EmmaCane.com